Roselle Graskey & Cheyne Curry

THE RESISTANCE

BOOK TWO
OF tHE
SANCTUARY SERIES

I0680260

BY

ROSELLE GRASKEY

AND

CHEYNE CURRY

Bossy Pants Books

THE RESISTANCE

DEDICATIONS

From Roselle Graskey:

To my wife Allison. Without you this could not be possible. You are my soul, my sweetheart, my home and my love.

From Cheyne Curry:

For Team Maguire and Women Warriors everywhere.

For Terri Marwood

And, always, for Paladin

**ALSO WRITTEN
BY CHEYNE CURRY AND
COMING SOON FROM BOSSY PANTS BOOKS:**

Clandestine
The Tropic of Hunter
Renegade
The End - Book One of The Sanctuary
Series (co-written by Roselle Graskey
and Cheyne Curry)

Coming Soon!

Permission To Recover

THE RESISTANCE

BOOK TWO
OF tHE
Sanctuary SERIES

BY

ROSELLE GRASKEY

AND

CHEYNE CURRY

Bossy Pants Books

NOTE: If you purchased this book without a cover, you should be aware that it is stolen property. It was reported as "unsold and destroyed" to the publisher, and neither the author nor the publisher has received any payment for this "stripped book."

This is a work of fiction. All characters, locales and events are either products of the author's imagination or are used fictitiously.

THE RESISTANCE

Copyright © 2019 by Roselle Graskey & Cheyne Curry
www.cheynecurry.com

All rights reserved. No part of this book may be reproduced in any manner whatsoever without written permission from the publisher, save for brief quotations used in critical articles or reviews.

Front and Back Cover design by Karen D. Badger

A Bossy Pants Book
Published by Bossy Pants Books
Columbus, Ohio 43229
bossypantsbooks@gmail.com

ISBN-10: 1-945124-04-0
ISBN-13: 978-1-945124-04-4

First Edition, March, 2019

Printed in the United States of America and in the United Kingdom

ACKNOWLEDGMENTS

Roselle would love to acknowledge the following people:

To our fans. Thank you for being so very patient with us.

Cheyne for being an excellent writing partner.

Brenda for letting Cheyne come out and play with me.

Karen Badger and Bliss, for everything.

Day Peterson for suffering through the manuscript. You always make us look good. Let me know where to send the wine and chocolates.

Marie Logan who keeps up with the right nudges. Yes, that's a good thing.

Ms. M for letting us borrow you.

Cheyne would love to acknowledge the following people:

Cheyne would love to acknowledge the following people:

Brenda Barton, my wife, my better half, my life. Your support and encouragement know no bounds. You are my champion and I love you with all my heart and soul.

Roselle Graskey for having the same mindset and warped sense of humor.

Karen Badger and Bliss (Badger Bliss Books) for all their help, time and effort dedicated to making all this a possibility.

Karen Badger for the cover/back cover art.

Day Peterson for her patience and mad skillz.

Allison Mugnier for her patience and accounting prowess.

Barb Coles and Linda Daniels for always stepping up. You both will always have a special place in my heart.

Chris Westfield, M.E. Logan, Renae Hunt and Brenda for their proofreading, input and pep talks.

CHaptER OnE

Branna Maguire, a wiry woman of average height, with closely cropped, dark hair and eyes brimming with intelligence, stood in her barracks room at ramrod attention. Without appearing to do so, she examined the high level American dignitary who had attended her graduation from the Irish Defense Forces Army Ranger Wing Special Forces School. In her estimation, he was rather ordinary looking, despite his dark charcoal suit and highbrow title.

She wondered what the hell he was doing all the way over in County Kildare, Ireland at Camp Curragh. And, more specifically, why he had requested an audience with just her, taking her away from her hard earned graduation, her passing out ceremony. Perhaps his mission was to get her kicked out of this army, as well. If that was the case, they were there alone and, hey, accidents could happen.

His eyes locked on her. "I understand you graduated second in your class. Most impressive, Staff Sergeant." He sounded almost pleasant. "And please relax."

"Sir, with all due respect, you are Chief of Staff to the President. I am required to maintain military discipline in the presence of the representative of the President of the United States," she snapped out in her best parade ground voice, trying not to sound too much as if she was correcting a small child.

"And the fact that the current administration supported hanging you out to dry has nothing to do with the likelihood that you hate my guts by proxy." David Segundo's smile seemed sincere.

"I have no political opinion, Sir."

He walked around her slowly. "Now, that's both true and not true, and we both know it. I can see what's in your eyes,

Sergeant, even if your face is frozen in neutral." He exhaled, *a long, slow sigh. "I'm going to say something to you which, if repeated in the wrong circles, will get me killed." His voice was both somber and honest. "I am a man, not a politician, who loves his country above his party."*

He stood in front of her, eye to eye. "The President is not who I thought, believed, him to be. As Chief of Staff, I'm a lot like living room furniture: they forget I'm there until they need me."

Staff Sergeant Maguire maintained her fixed gaze. "And I'm going to guess you also record everything you hear, every conversation you have. You don't strike me as a stupid man. Which is why, Sir, I am going to say again, I have no political opinion, Sir."

He lost his patience. "Damn it, Maguire! I'm not recording this! I am not stupid and I am not trying to set you up, I'm trying to save my damn country from being parceled out to the Russians and the Religious Right!"

"We call that baiting. You'll have to do better than that, Sir." She smiled thinly.

"No, actually baiting is what the President had certain alphabet agencies do to North Korea in order to get them to jump. And they did it so damned well that China couldn't interfere without looking like they set everything into motion." He took a deep breath and let it out. "Do you have any idea why we really went to war with Korea?"

"Mr. Segundo, I just fight the wars, I don't ask who pissed off whom in order to get there."

"Matthew 24:33: 'So likewise, when ye shall see these things, know that it is near, even at the doors.' Sound familiar? The President is willing to give the Religious Right their End of Times, and he's willing to give the Russians what they want in order to secure complete shared control over every other country in the world." His voice was steady, but laced with anger. "I am asking you to help me stop this. I know the Irish have offered you a place in their Defense Forces. I am asking you to serve the United States again."

Finally surrendering some of her strict military bearing,

Maguire blinked at him and laughed. "There are only three people who know that offer was made to me." She shook her head. "So, who's the loudmouth?"

"Someone who is smart enough to understand that it is not just America at risk, but Ireland, Antarctica, Zimbabwe... Everyone. Every country in the whole damn world!"

"Maybe, Mr. Segundo, just maybe you should reap what you have sown. You who helped elect him, and them that voted for him or voted against his main opposition." Maguire glared at him. "Maybe I have had enough of your shite wars to not give a damn what happens to all of you." She drew in a deep breath. "And maybe other countries have earned what will happen to them. I didn't see them standing up to the president. Still don't."

Segundo blinked repeatedly and then pointedly checked his watch. "I don't have the time I need to convince you. Officially, you have been congratulated on an accomplishment that brings great honor to the Military Police Corps and the United States Army. If asked, I will admit that our private exchange was as expected and that you still bear resentment towards those who you believe should have moved more expeditiously to relieve your element.

"Unofficially, and to those in my column, I will say that I have hope that you will rethink your current position. We need you, Staff Sergeant Maguire." He removed a card from the pocket his suit coat and pushed it into her right hand. "This is your appointment with the Irish immigration officer. General O'Keefe asked me to give it to you."

Maguire switched the card to her left hand and re-assumed the position of Attention. Feeling he didn't deserve her best protocol, she rendered a less-than-sharp salute with her right hand. "Thank you for coming, Sir," she snapped loudly, and then lowered her salute. After he left her room, she stared down at the business card that bore the seal of the President of the United States.

CHAPTER TWO

The sound of the bedroom door opening nudged Maguire out of her reminiscences. They had taken place four years earlier, and, true to Segundo's dire prediction, the entire world had been changed since then.

Devon Prescott shuffled into the office area, rubbing the sleep from her eyes. "What the hell, Maguire?" Prescott was a stocky woman in her late thirties, not unattractive but neither was she blessed with any outstanding or distinguishing features. She looked over at Rachel Noble, who had just finished pouring water into the coffeemaker. "Coffee? We just barely got to sleep." Prescott refocused on Maguire, who was seated at the table. "Why aren't you on your way to…wherever it was you were going?"

Maguire smirked. "I could say I'm sorry that I interrupted whatever was going on here, but I'm not. Not even shocked, really."

"Fuck you." Prescott stifled a yawn. She reached into a cupboard and took out three coffee mugs. "Now, what's going on? Why are you back?"

***

Rooted to their seats, the two women stared at Maguire with stunned expressions, coffee untouched in the cups in front of them. Over the past hour, Maguire had recounted what she knew about Operation Jaded Right, the purpose of the planned attack that had caused most areas of the world to be blown back into the Stone Age, and the meaning of Trodaí. She explained the coded message from Dr. Madras and revealed the involvement of the White House Chief of

Staff, David Segundo. When she had finished, the coffee wasn't the only thing in the room that was cold.

Prescott shivered. "That's…that's nuts. That's insane." She looked into Maguire's eyes and knew the ultimate soldier was telling the truth. Her eyes swept toward Noble, who had a knowing sneer on her face. "What?"

Noble shook her head as she stood up and moved to the coffeepot. She dumped her cold coffee into the sink and refilled the mug with hot, brought the cup to her lips, blew on the liquid, and then took a sip.

"You don't seem at all surprised." Prescott's tone was part question, part accusation.

"I'm not. There have been plans in place for installing a shadow government for nearly 50 years," Noble said. "Certain elements have been waiting for an event like this so that they could conquer whatever was left of the country and then function with complete autonomy beyond congressional oversight. They would suspend the Constitution, invoke martial law, and imprison anyone who dared to stand against them. When a world-wide catastrophe didn't happen as a result of the predictable posturing of world governments, it makes sense they would have had to create the necessary scenario to trigger events."

"Wait…but…the death and destruction…"

"Collateral damage," Maguire said.

"Exactly." Noble retook her seat. "The ends justify the means, especially for the greedy, soulless bastards who stand to benefit from such treachery."

"But how do they benefit? Everything is gone, either destroyed or uninhabitable," Prescott said, her voice rising with disbelief and frustration.

"It doesn't matter to them. I don't know what their ultimate strategy is…yet," Maguire said, "but I need to get to Dr. Madras, as she seems to be the linchpin that will bring us all together to formulate some kind of plan of resistance. There has to be a reason we were all trained and then psy-opsed."

"Absolutely," Noble agreed. "And there is a reason particular people were selected to perform certain tasks. I would hazard a guess that you are all experts in specific fields of operation or hands-on in tactical spheres of proficiency and knowledge." Noble couldn't disguise the hint of melancholy that colored her expression.

"What's the matter, Noble? Upset you weren't one of the chosen?" There was no ridicule in Maguire's voice. She was sincerely curious about Noble's response.

Noble appeared to understand what Maguire was asking. "Not really. I've had my time in the spotlight. I'm getting way too old for that shit now. I am perfectly happy to stay in the background and be one with all the support units." She studied Maguire. "But you…" She hesitated, then smiled. "It's your time now. Even if you didn't have your exceptional training, you have the instincts and, it seems, a natural gift for strategic thinking and survival. Segundo was smart and right to recognize your potential. I could happily live out the rest of my life just being caretaker of this sanctuary, but you, *you* are destined for something much more important and distinguished. If we are to survive, it will be the Maguires of the world who take us there."

Prescott rolled her eyes. "I think I'm going to puke."

Maguire looked at Noble, clearly shocked. "Me too."

***

"All the time you thought you were in counter-terrorism training, you were really in a special forces group of…of what? Shadow stalkers?" Prescott asked Maguire.

Maguire chuckled. "Shadow stalkers don't exist. They were the boogeymen used to scare the communists."

"Shadow stalkers. I haven't heard that term in years," Noble said. "I didn't think the SOG existed as such anymore. It was effectively replaced by Seal Team 6, Delta Force, and others like that, wasn't it?"

"It was a special operations group, but not called the SOG," Maguire answered. "The SOG, I believe, still exists— well, it did exist, and it had a specific purpose, but that was more like the US Marshal responsibilities of guarding, protecting, and handling protected witnesses. They still went to Camp Beauregard in Louisiana for training. Our training was at the old Fort Irwin site in the desert of California for the first half, and then at the decommissioned Camp Hale in the mountains of Colorado."

"Ah, yes, the 10th Mountain Division trained there during World War II." Noble rubbed her chin. "Did they teach you combat tactics on skis?"

"No. We were there for four weeks in the summer. The nights were definitely freezing, but the training was more about being on that kind of terrain than any specific strategy like a ski corps," Maguire said.

"Did you know that Camp Hale also served as a POW camp? It held a couple hundred of the most irredeemable members of Rommel's Afrika Corps," Noble added.

"Yes, we were told that. Also, that two of them escaped to Mexico with the help of an Army private who was supposed to be guarding them." Maguire took another swallow from the tumbler of Jameson's that Noble had slid over to her. She cradled the glass as though it was a lifeline. "Jesus Christ. We *knew* about the possibility of internal sabotage." Maguire shook her head. "We trained to prevent it, and we couldn't even do that."

"Maybe you weren't," Prescott spoke up. "Maybe you were trained for exactly what you are about to do." She had their attention. "Maybe Segundo knew there was no stopping the plan once it had been put in motion, which is why he had you all sent to 'safe' locations all over the country—so that you could survive and train others, build a resistance army, and kill all of the traitors."

CHAPTER THREE

Noble roused two of her best topographers and got them working on laying out a viable route to Yakima, Washington. She also plugged into satellite images of the terrain and helped point out possibilities of what Maguire might or might not be facing on her journey to the Northwest. They had been at it for several hours, trying to gather updated intel on access roads and design the most direct, most easily traversable route to where Dr. Madras was currently staying, when Noble called a break.

While everyone else took a breather, Maguire stayed in the room and studied the wall map. It was marked with symbols and numbers that indicated difficulty of passage, from undemanding to impossible. She needed to memorize the best route for her to follow, and this cartogram incorporated all of the available reconnaissance to help get her to her goal.

It looked as if her best course would be to follow the Salmon River to the Snake River to the Yakima River, and from there she would be on the edge of the Yakima Training Center where Madras was supposed to be holed up in a vacation cabin.

"So, what do you think, Maguire?" Prescott asked as she came back into the office. "Aside from getting to Madras without being detected, what do you think is going to be the most challenging element of this new mission?"

Without missing a beat, still studying the map, Maguire said, "Saying goodbye to Anna again."

***

Noble took a step back from the calculations displayed on the whiteboard, corkboard, and wall. "It looks like we have planned out as much as we can prepare for, Maguire."

Maguire's finger touched the map and traced the route that was outlined in blue. "With decent weather and no dire obstacles, I can probably get to Yakima in three days."

"Three days?" Prescott exclaimed. "Who do you think you are, The Flash?"

"The travel route is all along the rivers and the locks that connect them. I can appropriate some kind of boat, even if it's a rowboat, and follow the current. It could take longer, five days at the outside, but I really don't think it will."

"And you'll take Prescott with you," Noble stated.

Maguire's and Prescott's heads simultaneously snapped up and they chorused, "What?"

"I said, you will take Prescott with you."

"No fecking way!" Maguire shook her head vigorously.

"And shouldn't I have a say about this?" Prescott interjected.

"I don't take orders from you, Noble," Maguire reminded her evenly.

Noble sighed. "I didn't mean to make it sound like an order. Look, regardless of how much time you have spent here and how much time you have spent training your elite force, no one here knows you better than Prescott. No one has had actual, real world experience with you except Prescott. This can't be a training mission. It's too important."

"I'm going alone," Maguire stated flatly.

Noble drew her hand through her short, gray hair. "Look…I get it, Maguire, I do. You're pissed at me, and you have every right to be. I fucked up. There. Is that what you wanted to hear? Okay, I admit it. I fucked up!"

"Now why doesn't that make me feel any better?"

"Because I can't bring Baumer back. So, to punish me, you'll defy me and reject whatever I suggest. I get it. Put the past aside and focus on the realities of the here-and-now. You can't go alone. What if something were to happen to you and you couldn't get to Madras?"

"If I can't get to her and bring her back, she won't get

here. If something happens to me, that will mean anybody with me is already dead."

"Which speaks directly to why I shouldn't go with her," Prescott said. "Besides, someone needs to be here for Anna."

"Anna's doing just fine," Noble said. "She is adjusting, and she's safe. You and she aren't exactly best pals; I'm sure she'll survive without you."

Maguire noticed the flicker of...something...that crossed Prescott's visage. She'd have to ask her about that later. "I work better solo," she insisted, returning to the topic of conversation.

"Well, this is no longer just about you, Maguire," Noble said firmly.

***

Maguire braced Prescott outside Noble's office. "Inside, you said you needed to be here for Anna. I thought she was taking care of herself now. What haven't you told me? Are you two...?" Maguire's eyes narrowed. "Since you're fucking Noble, you had better not be playing Anna," she warned.

"No! No, I honestly don't believe her crush will amount to anything. That's just curiosity, and maybe some confusion. It's not that." Prescott looked at the floor. " It's...uh...Carrie."

Maguire turned Prescott to face her. Her tone was a dangerous growl as she demanded, "What about Carrie?"

Prescott held up a hand. "Now hold on. I took care of it, but my concern is that if both of us are gone, there'll be no one to police Carrie's predatory behavior towards Anna."

"If you believe there is still an issue, then you didn't take care of anything." Maguire took a deep breath. "What did Carrie do?"

***

Carrie awoke to find Maguire sitting on the chair opposite her bed. She sat up quickly, reaching for her pistol.

Maguire held up the weapon. "Looking for this?"

"Give me back my gun," Carrie demanded. "And what are you doing here, anyway? You're supposed to be gone."

Maguire smiled patiently and cleared the Beretta M9 as she spoke. "Why I am back is none of your concern. That part has nothing to do with you. Fortunately for you." She depressed the magazine release button and the full clip fell into the boonie hat on her lap. "As to why I am here, in your bedroom, it's to have a little chat." She pulled the slide to the rear, removed a chambered round, and dropped the bullet into her shirt pocket. She then pushed the slide stop up, locking it in place, and looked into the chamber to ensure it was empty. "I understand you've been sniffing around Anna and your attentions are not welcome." Maguire released the slide and let it snap forward. "Anna is off-limits to you." She pressed the disassembly lever button with her forefinger, then rotated that lever downward until it stopped.

"God, what is it with you and Prescott? Anna is not your property," Carrie spat. "She is an adult who can make her own choices."

Pulling the slide and barrel assembly forward, Maguire removed it from the receiver. "So long as it is her choice and not a result of coercion. According to Prescott, it didn't appear as if you were giving Anna much of an option." Maguire carefully compressed the recoil spring and spring guide while lifting and extracting them. She then separated the parts, inspected them, and placed them in the hat.

"Anna tell you that, or just Prescott?" A hint of cockiness had returned to Carrie's tone.

Maguire stopped disassembling the weapon and looked directly at Carrie. "Do you want me to ask Anna to tell me exactly how violated she felt by your behavior? Do you have a death wish?" When Carrie shook her head, Maguire went back to her task. She pushed in on the locking block plunger while forcing the barrel forward slightly, then lifted and removed the assemblies from the slide. She studied the items in her hat with disgust. "Jaysus, Carrie, have you ever cleaned this thing? When was the last time it was fired?"

A flush of embarrassment rose to her face. "I've, um,

never actually fired it."

Maguire's mouth dropped open. "Well, no wonder it's a pigsty. Can it even shoot?"

"Of course," Carrie said indignantly.

"Are you sure?" Maguire leaned forward and held the components out toward Carrie. "This is your lifeline. You have to treat it with respect. One aspect of that is to ensure it is always in proper working condition. You need to practice with it, get to know its quirks and benefits. Get to know your strengths and weaknesses in shooting. You need to take it apart after every time you use it and wipe it free of gummed oil, dirt, dust, and carbon buildup. You have to pay particular attention to the hard to reach areas like the bolt face, guide rails on the receiver, grooves on the slide." Maguire placed all of the pieces into the side utility pocket in her pants, then stood up.

"Wait, where are you going? Give me back my gun!" Carrie started to get out of bed, but froze when Maguire took two steps toward her.

"I'm turning this mess over to Noble and telling her why I took it away from you. You can explain to her why you're so arrogant that you treat it like a shiny accessory instead of a deadly weapon that may have to be used to save her life at some point." She leaned in closer and her voice took on a quiet, deadly tone. "If you ever go near Anna again, I will come back for you. And you'll never know where I'll be or when I will be there. If you ever touch her again, I will hurt you, and I will make it a hurt that never goes away as a permanent reminder of what you did. Are we clear on that, Carrie?"

Carrie quailed beneath Maguire's intense expression, and she shifted further back on her bed before she muttered, "Yes, we're clear."

As soon as Maguire moved away and stepped over the threshold, she heard Carrie's cot springs squeak, indicating Carrie had left the bed.

Maguire stepped back inside Carrie's bedroom and saw her opening her closet door. "And don't bother going for your

M16 to think you can use it to scare me. You'll find that broken down into parts, too, in your top drawer. You want to use it, you're going to have to put it back together first. If you don't know how, you can go ask anyone in the militia for help. Preferably after you have cleaned it."

CHAPTER FOUR

Anna got out of bed slowly. She was not really looking forward to the days ahead. With Maguire off on her own to who knew where, she could feel emptiness enveloping her. First Szabo, then Baumer, and now Maguire. Maguire wasn't dead, but in this new world, with her gone from Sanctuary, she might as well be. It wasn't as if there was any convenient rapid transportation to get Maguire back for a visit anytime soon, if at all. Well, there was still Doc in town, and she had Prescott.

Anna rubbed her eyes, still burning and sore from crying all afternoon and most of the night before. She scrubbed her face with her hands as though that would wipe everything away and make her feel better. It didn't. She released a deep sigh as she looked down at herself. She had not even changed out of the clothes she had been wearing the day before. Studying her reflection in the mirror, she saw an exhausted, rumpled mess. With a shrug, she walked out of her room toward the kitchenette.

Passing Maguire's empty room, tears stung her eyes again. Anna took a deep breath to get her emotions under control. She needed to go to the agricultural building to get some fresh eggs for the day, not that she felt much like eating, but she knew if she waited too long, there wouldn't be any left and she might be hungry later. In the tiny kitchen, she poured herself a glass of water and then drank it slowly, trying to focus on something other than the feeling of utter emptiness in the pit of her stomach. When she walked into the small living area, she stopped dead in her tracks.

"'Bout time you got up, dearlin'." Maguire was seated on the couch, but she stood up and held out four eggs. "I'm

14

starving, how about you?"

Anna was momentarily speechless, then tripped over her tongue trying to express several thoughts at once, which came out sounding like what Jess had once called *word salad*. "Mags!" In two steps, she was in Maguire's arms, holding onto her for all she was worth.

At least a full minute passed before Maguire said, "Glad to see you, too, but I think you just broke all the eggs."

Anna stepped back and saw messy yolks and egg whites dripping down the fronts of them both. "I don't care. I'll gladly sacrifice my breakfast for this moment." She was crying again, but in much better spirits. "What happened? Why are you back?"

"Interesting development, that," Maguire said. "At least tell me we have some coffee left."

"We do."

"Well, then, let's make some and settle in for a bit."

***

Both women had changed and washed the egg off of their shirts, and were back in the kitchenette. Anna placed both articles of clothing over the back railing to dry in the sun.

After the coffee was poured, Anna and Maguire sat down at the small table and shared the rest of the homemade bread Anna had baked two days earlier in one of the communal clay ovens.

"So, Mags, why are you back? And are you here to stay?" Anna's voice held the lilt of hope.

"Unfortunately, no. I have a new mission that's going to take both Prescott and me away for a month or so."

Anna's expression was crestfallen. "Prescott's leaving too?"

"Not my choice either, kiddo, but Noble made a good point about practiced teamwork."

"I'm part of the team. Can I go?"

For a moment, Maguire actually considered the request, then she grimaced. "That wouldn't be a good idea. We won't be dealing with the likes of what we've already encountered. You'll be much safer here."

"Are you sure?" Anna asked skeptically.

"If you're worried about Carrie, I had a little chat with her this morning."

"And Prescott had a little chat with her before. With both of you gone, I don't think she'll be concerned about any suggestions either of you made."

Maguire sipped her coffee and contemplated Anna's situation. "Time to take your power back, Anna. You attended quite a few of the self-defense training classes I conducted. Lisa Jennings is still teaching them, if you need a refresher. I don't want you to be afraid in a place you are now calling home. Carrie talks the talk, but cannot walk the walk. If she can't take 'no' for an answer, you need to remind her what the word 'no' feels like."

"But Noble doesn't like it when there are physical altercations in her compound."

"Know what Noble likes even worse? Anyone behaving predatorily toward the women in her safe haven."

"But it's *Carrie*."

"Yes, and Noble is going to have a not-so-nice little chat with her tomorrow. Until we came along, I don't think Noble had any idea that Carrie was the fuck up she actually is. Carrie used her position in the ranks to bully everyone into thinking Noble would protect her, regardless of what she did. Carrie's beginning to realize that is not so. With Noble's reinforcement, Carrie is about to have the wind taken right out of her sails."

"But if there is no one to stay on Noble to stay on Carrie because you two are gone, what makes you think her sails will stay windless?"

"As much as I am not a friend of Noble's, despite what she did in the LT's situation, I believe that she is a principled person, especially when it comes to protecting women. And with both Prescott and me warning her about Carrie's behavior, she has to take it seriously."

Anna hesitated and then said, "It still won't be the same

without either of you here."

"You can always go into town and live with Doc. He'd be glad to have your company, and I'm sure he would love to continue to train you to be his medical assistant." Maguire finished her coffee. "I'd say try to stick it out here first, because you do have the safeguard of these walls and Noble's know-how. But if Carrie or anyone else makes it impossible for you to stay, kick their ass and then move into Dodge." She rose from the chair and moved to the sink to rinse her mug. "Anna, you have come through so much more, survived so much more than the majority of these women have, or hopefully ever will have to. Don't give Carrie or anyone else power over you. Just don't allow it. You're strong and capable, and you are a survivor. Always remember that."

***

It was dusk, and Maguire was itching to get on the trail. She had taken a short but deep nap, and woke up mentally refreshed and immediately alert. She took a quick shower and dressed in a clean pair of BDUs which Anna had washed and dried for her. Her rucksack had not been unpacked from her intended departure two days earlier, so it was ready to go. Before she left Noble's cabin, she gathered all of the maps and information that had been prepared. With Anna in tow, so as to not miss her final goodbyes again, Maguire crossed the compound and knocked on Prescott's door.

"Come in!" Prescott hollered, sounding out of breath.

"You better not tell me you aren't ready," Maguire yelled, holding the door open for Anna.

"I overslept," Prescott admitted as she rolled up a poncho to add to her half-packed duffel. "This is my second," she said, stowing the waterproof item. "You said two each, right?"

"Right." Maguire looked around at the mess that was Prescott's bedroom. "We're entering rain country, and if we connect them to make a shelter, we can hopefully stay dry when we need to." She pointed at an entrenching tool leaning against the bedpost. "You're taking that?"

"I shouldn't?"

"It's your choice, but it will add weight. By making sure the ponchos are angled correctly, we shouldn't need it."

"Can I do anything to help?" Anna asked Prescott.

"Nope. I'm almost done. Thank you, though. Oh, wait, since I'm not sure how long we will be gone, there are a few things in the kitchen you might as well take home with you."

"Okay. I'll get them when you're ready to leave."

"Are you sure you want to come with us to the gate?" Maguire asked Anna. "It might be easier to give hugs here and—"

"Mags," Anna said sternly, "I am walking you two to the gate." Her tone brooked no argument.

Prescott looked up, eyes flitting back and forth between Anna and Maguire. "Guess she told you," she said to Maguire, then she chuckled and went back to her packing.

A slight grin curled the corner of Maguire's mouth. "I guess she did." She winked at Anna and refocused on Prescott. "Get that Limey ass moving, Prescott. We're already off schedule."

Prescott stuffed more items into her pack as she rolled her eyes. "What? By five minutes?"

"Seven minutes and twenty-two seconds, and flapping your jaws is making it longer."

Prescott began to secure her duffel. "This is going to be so much fun, this trip with you."

"I know. Try to restrain your elation and let's get going."

***

Approximately two hours after she had been advised by the front gate of Maguire and Prescott's departure, Rachel Noble knocked on the door of the small cabin that Maguire had shared with Baumer and Anna. She waited for the single remaining occupant to answer.

The wooden front door opened with a creak and Anna stood behind the inside screen door, looking sleepy and forlorn. She glared at Noble.

"Good morning, Anna," Noble said with forced cheerfulness. She knew she was not Anna's favorite person and tried not to sound like her typical, gruff self.

"Mmph," Anna mumbled, not yet fully awake.

"I wonder if I could talk to you about something."

"Mmph," Anna responded, folding her arms over her chest.

"Inside."

Anna yawned and turned away, leaving the door open. Noble took that as an invitation and entered the cabin. "I'm guessing you don't have any coffee made."

"Nope. You're welcome to make some, though."

At least she's forming words and making sentences now. Noble needed to keep the visit short, so decided she didn't want to take the time for coffee. "I have a favor to ask you."

Anna rubbed her eyes, focused on Noble, then shook her head. "Carrie's your problem to deal with, and no, I will not ignore her just to get along here. Mags and Prescott said—"

"This is not about Carrie. I did speak with Maguire and Prescott regarding that situation, and I will handle it. This is more personal. This is about my granddaughter."

Anna's eyes flashed with an anger Noble had not previously seen in her. This was going to be a lot harder than she had thought.

* * *

Maguire's goal was to reach the westernmost territory of the Idaho Panhandle without incident by early afternoon. Maguire and Prescott intended to travel "as the crow flies" as much as possible without adding more elevation or distance to their trek. Her navigation was mapped out to keep them parallel to state routes and waterways, while avoiding areas that were known to be populous or even just inhabited to any extent.

Maguire had noted that Prescott had remained unusually quiet thus far into their trip. Her guess was that either she was still stewing over having to be there at all, or she recognized that talking would use up energy that they needed to traverse the miles. Either way, Maguire was grateful.

Maguire hoped to cross over the Idaho state line to Clarkston, Washington by nightfall. A lot of that territory was open area. Staying concealed would require a concerted effort. As they had learned with Joseph Red Horse, they never knew who was watching or how.

Chapter Five

Anna walked into Noble's office and immediately noted the young girl seated in front of Nobel's desk. There was no mistaking the resemblance between the two or the expression of pure disgust on the face of the younger. Unlike a lot of the females in the compound, the girl's hair was long and tied away from her face in a light brown braid. Freckles spattered her cheeks and the bridge of her nose, and the girl's hazel eyes reflected practiced disinterest.

"Are we ready?" Anna delivered the question with a smile she didn't really feel.

"Anna, Angel. Angel, this is Anna."

"Whatever," the girl muttered.

"I'm not all that thrilled about you, either," Anna shot back at Angel, then glanced at Noble, whose left eyebrow had found a space somewhere near her hairline.

"You've wanted to do more around here, well, this is the best solution I can come up with right now," Noble told Anna.

"I wanted to shadow Noreen and your healers to hopefully be able to help out here," Anna corrected. "I never said I wanted to be a babysitter."

Angel instantly looked insulted. "I don't need a babysitter!"

"Angel, we are not going to discuss this again," Noble admonished. "You don't know how to be productive with your time, which means others, including me, have to spend precious hours playing hide-and-seek with you. Now you will either spend a few hours with Anna while I am at meetings, or you will be confined to my residence with guards at the door."

"You can't make me do that, Gram," Angel retorted with a sneer.

"I'm afraid I can, little girl, and I'm getting really fed up with this new attitude of yours. You either spend time with Anna, or you're grounded." She watched Angel roll her eyes and look away. Noble shook her head and said to Anna. "I have to go. Don't kill each other." With that and a worried glance back, she left the office.

Anna counted to twenty-five in her head and then took a seat next to Angel, who blatantly ignored her. She counted to twenty-five again.

"I don't need a babysitter," Angel repeated, her expression never changing.

"No?" Anna's tone was even. "So, if I wasn't here, what would you be doing with your time?"

Angel shrugged a shoulder. "I don't know."

"Well today you are going to find out." Anna stood. "First stop is the infirmary, to see if Noreen needs anything. After that, it's over to the barn to walk some of the horses."

"I'm not slave labor, you know." Her tone was laced with teenaged disgust.

"No one gets a free ride anymore," Anna answered in the most reasonable tone she could muster. "Not even thirteen-year-olds. Let's move."

For a long moment Angel was motionless, then she slithered out of her seat and stood up. A long-suffering sigh signaled that she was bowing to the pressure. "Whatever."

***

Noble watched the six women enter the conference room of the underground silo. They were the governing group department heads and the two spokeswomen for the group of investors. Though she was not looking forward to this discussion and wanted to get it over with, Noble maintained an expression of patience. Finally, each woman had selected a beverage and taken a seat around the table.

"Ladies, thank you for coming so quickly. I apologize for

the short notice. I will try not to take up too much of your time. We all have things to do, and I'm afraid I'm going to add to all of our burdens." She leaned forward in her seat and looked at each of them, one at a time. "We have come far since our world was destroyed, but the danger is not over. Intelligence has come to light that the destruction was deliberate, and for a purpose which, quite honestly is even more horrific than the destruction itself."

Brittany Warrens leaned back in her seat. "What could be more horrific than practically being blown back into the Stone Age?"

The thin blonde held herself with an air of subtle arrogance, and Noble had to remind herself that Warrens did actually work hard on occasion. "Right now, without confirmation, we can only guess that survivors are to be used as a slave labor force for those who have dropped us into this hell," Noble answered honestly.

Warrens laughed. "C'mon, Rachel, another conspiracy theory?"

Noble's eyes drilled into the woman. "I do believe, Brittany, that you also called my reasoning for establishing this sanctuary a conspiracy theory when your mother decided to invest." The verbal reminder of who held the purse strings was deliberate. "It's no longer a theory when an event actually happens," she snapped, then took a breath. "Two members of our young army are en route to confirm this *theory*. It could take a week to ten days for them to return, and I didn't build my career by wasting time. To that end, department heads, please come up with emergency plans to lock down again on a moment's notice."

"Rachel," the head of Communications interrupted, "do you mean longer term lockdown than what we just went through?"

Noble nodded. "It has the potential to be extremely long term. I will have more information when our personnel return. Think worst case, and hope for better." She turned back to Warrens. "Brittany," she slid a file across the desk, "please present this to your organization."

Warrens rolled her eyes. "And tell them what?"

Noble ground her teeth. "Tell them that attack might not be over."

***

The infirmary staff and the horse grooms did not need any assistance from Anna and Angel, as most of the chores were either nearly completed or concluded by the time they got to each facility. And Anna had tolerated Angel's whining and posing for as long as she could. She halted so quickly that the teenager slammed into Anna's back. Angel stumbled and fell on her butt, yelling in startled, then indignant outrage. Anna reached down and hauled the girl up by her shirt collar, and didn't let go.

"You know what, your Highness?" Anna took a deep breath. "I am really sick of your bad mouthing everything and everyone. It's 'everyone' against you." She tugged hard enough that Angel didn't have a choice about following. It was that or be dragged.

With Angel sputtering in protest the entire way, both were soaked with sweat when they eventually reached a particular section of the riverbank. Anna put her hands on Angel's shoulders and physically turned her to face the bank. "Two weeks ago, you decided to run off. This is the spot." Anna nudged the girl forward toward a caved-in area. "Take a look, or just jump on down."

"What?" Angel's voice held confusion.

"You are so convinced that no one gives a damn about you? Do you remember the last time you played hide-and-go-seek? Everyone in Sanctuary dropped everything to look for you."

"That's not special. Everyone has to. My grandmother gets mad if they don't." The reply was half sarcasm, half smug, and totally devoid of any remorse.

Anna barely stopped herself from backhanding the girl. "Jessica Baumer – my friend – died because of your stupid, attention-seeking game playing, and apparently that doesn't bother you a bit." Angel quietly looked at the ground, which prompted Anna to think that maybe there was a shred of a conscience in there after all. Anna pointed to a spot near where Angel's gaze was directed. "This is where she got bit by a venomous spider. Jess didn't realize she'd been bitten, because when the bank came down, she landed on her butt, hard, right in the middle of poison ivy. She thought she was feeling sick because she was allergic to poison ivy. She died two mornings later." Anna didn't quite succeed at keeping the anger and condemnation out of her voice. "It's time you got it through your head that the world does not revolve around you. It never did, and it most certainly won't now."

"You don't know shit," the girl growled. "And you don't know me."

Anna's chuckle was not mocking. "Oh, sweetheart, you're me, nine years ago. I grew up second, sometimes fourth best at everything. My best friends, heck, some days my *only* friends, were our farm animals. If anyone saw me, it was because something had gone wrong. I may not know you, but trust me, your Highness, I *know* you."

"Whatever," Angel said again, but this time with less dismissiveness and more angst.

Anna made a point not to make a big deal of the tears glistening in the corners of Angel's eyes and decided to take a different approach. "Everyone assumes that you will someday take over for your grandma."

Angel lowered her head and nodded slowly.

"I bet no one has once asked you what you want." Anna recognized the softening expression on Angel's face when she lifted her head. "That happened to me, too," Anna admitted. "So, Angel...What *do* you want?"

Angel looked closely at the riverbank's edge before she flopped down on it. "I don't know anymore."

Anna studied the teenager, who had suddenly lost her false bravado. She also carefully checked the ground before she joined Angel. "Today doesn't have to be a negative experience, you know. You seem like you might actually have a lot to say. I'm a good listener, and I'm really not that much older than you." Her tone was soft and compassionate. "You seem pretty angry. Are you mad at your grandmother?"

Angel shrugged, using her shoulder to wipe a tear that had escaped. "She doesn't get it," Angel finally said, her voice so low that Anna had to lean in to hear her.

"What doesn't she get?"

Angel shrugged again, and stayed silent.

"How about you pretend I'm your grandmother, and you tell me exactly what's bothering you?"

Angel looked up sharply at Anna. "Why? You'll just run to her and tell her everything I say."

"That will depend on what you tell me. If you are intending on doing any harm to yourself or others, yes, I would tell her immediately. But if you're just frustrated about things, why not use me as a sounding board. Chances are, I've been through something similar."

"Oh, really? Is your mother dead? Is your father a rapist?" Angel spat out.

Anna recognized the venomous tone with which the words were said. Should she bring up to Angel that she was a rape survivor? She thought for a minute and then she said, "Yes, my mother is dead. As is my father and all my siblings. Everyone I knew before I met Baumer and the others are all dead. But your mom— She didn't die in the attack, did she?"

"No. She died from a drug overdose. I heard Gram say that she never recovered from the rape, which is how I came to be. So it's my fault that she died, and Gram blames me."

"Oh no, Angel, your Grandmother doesn't blame—"

"Yes, she does!" Angel yelled. "You don't know her!"

Anna waited until Angel had calmed down somewhat. "You're right. I don't know her. I only know what I've experienced since I've been here. Your grandmother has a lot of responsibility on her shoulders. And I'm sure she has even more now that we're all survivors. I have a feeling that maybe one of the issues is that she doesn't pay as much attention to you as she did before."

Angel shook her head. "She never really paid a lot of attention to me anyway. This place has always come first. We always lived with her, and after my mom died, Gram would palm me off on someone else, so she could work."

"How old were you when your mom died?"

"Eight."

"Did your mom pay a lot of attention to you? Spend a lot of time with you?"

"She slept a lot. Gram used to get angry with her, and she'd take me out of our place and bring me to work with her. Then Gram started getting other people to watch me. When we would go home, Mom would be out of it, but at night, she would always curl up with me and hold me. I miss that. Gram has never allowed me to do that with her."

"Did that make you feel rejected?"

"Well, yeah. Ever since Mom died, Gram's treated me differently, like she can't stand to be around me. She blames me."

Anna took in Angel's words and thought about them for a moment. "Maybe it hurts her, too, that your mom is no longer here. Maybe she's had just as hard a time as you and doesn't know how to talk to you about it. It seems to me that she loves you very much. She certainly gets frantic when you disappear. If she didn't care, why would she order everyone to stop what they're doing and immediately start looking for you?"

Angel shrugged again.

"When we were in the office, your grandmother said that this attitude of yours is new. That tells me there's something else, something recent that's bugging you. Want to tell me what that might be?"

"Why?" Angel looked at her. "Not like there's anything you can do about it."

"Try me. Maybe we can put our heads together and work something out."

"Why do you care?"

"Why don't you give me a reason to care?" Anna's tone did not echo the snotty quality of Angel's.

It took Angel a few moments of starts and stops before she finally was able to voice what she wanted to say. "She sent my friends away." Tears formed in the corners of her eyes, and this time they spilled down her cheeks. "My best friends are twins named Shaun and Dylan. We are the same age, and we all grew up playing together. A couple of months before you came, they were sent away. Their voices had started to change, and they hit that mark that Gram won't tolerate, so she sent them to the camp down the road." Angel's tears were flowing freely now. "I really miss them. They are like my brothers. I haven't been allowed to see them, and they haven't been allowed to come here, either. I've asked Gram if I can go with Christa—she's their mom—when she goes to see them, but Gram always says no. She said something about raging hormones and not trusting them around me now." She looked directly at Anna. "Shouldn't she be able to trust me?"

"She should, once you give her a reason to," Anna said gently. "By you running off and disappearing all the time or behaving like a brat, you haven't given her any reason to put that kind of faith in you. You aren't showing her that you are responsible enough to be trusted."

"I knew you'd side with her," Angel said bitterly.

"I'm not entirely siding with her," Anna corrected mildly. "Even though I understand why your grandmother sends all boys away, I'm not sure I entirely agree with her."

Angel looked back at Anna hopefully. "Really?"

"I understand why she does it and I think she sincerely believes it's for your own protection, but I also think she's doing you a disservice by keeping you away from your friends. There are a few girls around here your age. You're not friends with any of them?"

"They hate me. They think anything they say or do around me will get back to my gram."

"You know the rules, though, Angel, and you knew the boys' time was getting close. Did you think your grandmother wouldn't send them away because of your closeness to them?"

"I was hoping."

"If your grandmother had allowed Shaun and Dylan to stay, wouldn't that mean she'd have to change the rules for all the other boys?"

"Yeah, I guess so," Angel admitted reluctantly.

"I bet all of the boys who have been sent to the camp were not as nice as Shaun and Dylan, either."

"No. There was Eddie. He left a year before Shaun and Dylan. He was a bully. He was always being sent to my gram to be disciplined. He was really big for his age, and even though he's a year younger than Shaun and Dylan, he got sent away before them. Gram said he was too aggressive."

"So, let's use Eddie as an example. If Shaun and Dylan had been allowed to stay, what would stop Eddie's mom from asking your gram if Eddie could come back?"

"But Eddie always caused problems," Angel protested. "Shaun and Dylan never did anything."

"That doesn't mean Eddie's mom loves him any less than Shaun and Dylan's mom loves them. Your grandmother needs to be fair with everyone."

"She's not fair with me."

"I'm sure it feels that way but—" Anna saw Angel roll her eyes. "Angel, can I ask you a personal question?"

"Um…yeah, I guess."

"Have you started your period yet?"

"Why would you need to know that?"

"It could explain why your emotions are all over the place. I remember when I started my period, I was a walking ball of angst."

"How old were you when you started?"

"Twelve and a half."

Angel nodded. "I started about six months ago."

"The same time your grandmother sent your friends away?"

"Yeah."

Anna contemplated that and then said, "You know, Angel, I think your grandmother loves you so much that she doesn't want anything bad happen to you—in addition to what already has, that is—so she removes the temptation from the equation. I think she's afraid, not that the boys will intentionally hurt you, but that you'll all get curious and maybe start experimenting."

"Experimenting? With what? Drugs?"

"No. Sex."

"Sex?" Angel looked repulsed. "Yuck! Why would she think that? I told you, they are like my brothers. Ew!"

Anna grinned at Angel's reaction. "You may feel that way, but maybe Shaun or Dylan was starting to feel something else, more...romantic... toward you. I think that's what your grandmother feared. She doesn't want there to be any possibility that you would go through what your mom did." *Or what I did,* she thought but did not voice.

"Well, I don't feel that way about either of them. Shouldn't that make a difference?"

"Like I said, you need to give your grandmother a reason to be able to trust you. I tell you what. You start doing what she needs you to and stop these little hide-and-seek games for attention, and I will ask her if I can escort you to the camp so that you can visit Shaun and Dylan."

"Oh my God, really?" Angel said, excited. "You'd do that for me?"

"Not without an effort on your part to earn your grandmother's faith in you. And understand that I will not leave you unchaperoned." Anna suddenly found herself wrapped in a bear hug.

"You're the best, Anna." Angel gave Anna an extra squeeze.

"Let's not get ahead of ourselves, Angel. First, it will all depend on you and your behavior, and second, I cannot guarantee that your grandmother will go along with it."

"But you'll still ask her, right?"

Angel's entire demeanor had changed, and Anna liked this girl much better than spoiled, bratty Angel. "I will ask her when she tells me she's noticed a significant change in you."

"Promise?" Angel extended her pinkie finger.

Smiling, Anna latched on to Angel's pinkie with her own and nodded. "Promise."

Chapter Six

Maguire opened her weary eyes at the first sound of someone entering the mouth of the cave. Her hiding spot was well at the back, tucked under a tangled mess of long ago fallen rock which, while not overwhelmingly comfortable, was an improvement over many of her past sleeping arrangements. And, the rock would mask her presence and body heat. She remained motionless in the dark.

"Thank you, Steve." Segundo dropped his pack heavily and his bodyguard set down a larger duffle bag. "I'll be fine from here."

"Yes, Sir. I'll be parked by the ranger office."

Segundo sighed. "Steve…"

"Yes, Sir. Sorry. I am aware that you already know the drill."

The bodyguard sounded sheepish, and Segundo laughed. "Steve, you really need to learn to relax."

"Sir, you are Chief of Staff to the President. You know how many leftists would love to find out your location right now," he protested.

"Steve, the quickest way to let the opposition know where you're going is to bring an entire damned parade with you. I won't allow them to dictate when or where I go on vacation. As far as anyone is concerned, I'm at home unplugging from the world for a few days." Segundo's voice hardened. "Now, you may leave." His tone left no room for argument.

For several minutes after his Secret Service escort left, Segundo rummaged around, arranging things the way he wanted them, then he stepped out of the cave. He returned ten minutes later, dragging a tied bundle of firewood and kindling. He dropped the line of nylon rope and squatted to untie it. *"You can come out now, Sergeant. If you're here, that is."*

***

Maguire watched him closely as she slowly emerged from her space. She stalked him on silent feet, just for fun. *"Nice place you've got,"* she finally said, and watched with perverse pleasure as he twitched, then turned to face her.

"Thank you for meeting me."

She waved a hand around. *"All this cloak and dagger—"*

"Is better than being dead, Sergeant," he finished for her.

Maguire looked around the interior of the cave. She'd arrived during the middle of the night, and was more than ready for sleep. *"And this place is safe?"*

Segundo's laugh was soft. *"I don't actually enjoy camping or nature, Sergeant. I picked this place because of its high level of electromagnetic radiation. EMR is a wonderful thing if you don't want cell phones, recording devices, location bugs, and the like to work. Even walkie-talkies have issues here. I also insist on minimal security coverage on my vacations...to save taxpayer money, don't you know."*

"Veritable fecking saint," Maguire said dryly.

Segundo sighed. *"I know. I helped elect a destructive, power hungry child who ultimately destroys whatever he touches.*

"And?"

"And at first it was bluster, campaign-speak, promises everyone knows aren't going to be kept, but sound good to the base. Every politician does it. All sides." Segundo sucked in a breath and caught Maguire's gaze and held it. *"Initially, I sincerely bought into his and the party's patriot-speak, but he has gone so far beyond the pale I can hardly believe that he's serious. I cannot...will not sacrifice my country for his arrogance, his greed...their greed."*

"Who are they? The party?"

"No. Franklin and Petrushev." Segundo sat heavily on the ground.

"As in the most well-known Dominionist scam artist and the Russian president? Those two?"

"And Scholtz. The Triumvirate. They are planning something. I truly don't know exactly what it is, but in the digital recording I reviewed, they were discussing their 'power share'." He looked at Maguire again. "They were verbally carving up the world, Sergeant."

Maguire allowed that thought to sink in, and all she could do was blink. "Carving up? There's no way other world leaders would accept that."

"It won't matter. They can't stop anything if they're dead."

His words stopped Maguire cold. "You're serious."

"Serious enough to risk my life. The last two leaks in Petrushev's circle ended up with their brains blown out. Kind of hard to commit suicide with a shotgun blast to the back of the head, but 'officially' they committed suicide. I need your help."

Maguire watched him—his body language, which way his eyes twitched—and listened to what he wasn't saying. "Why me?"

"It would seem that you never quite know when to quit. God forbid that we can't stop whatever those three have planned, then that 'can't quit' thing that you have will be a necessary thing indeed. And, you will not be alone. There are others who can match your skills and mindset. You all will have to be the best hope for this country. Perhaps the world."

Maguire's chuckle was hard and cutting. "Other people wearing a uniform?"

Segundo nodded.

Maguire moved forward and dropped to one knee in front of him, her face inches from his. "Why didn't you pick country over party when it mattered? Now, yet again, uniforms have to come to the rescue." When he didn't answer, she leaned toward him and growled, "Why?"

He pulled his head away and dropped his gaze. "Power, damn it. And money. And the White House. I'm a minority, and I wanted my place in history. Anyone at this level of politics, if they tell you they don't want it, you can put money down that he or she is a liar." Segundo shook his head. "Scholz wasn't like this at the beginning. He was an ass when the campaign started, but you could talk some sense into him. It became impossible when Franklin became a top advisor and Petrushev backchanneled on board." He took a sip of water from his canteen. "The Democrats had been in power too long; we were losing our rights. If it had continued, the country would have gone down the Socialist road. I didn't want that; no Conservative wants that."

Maguire snorted. "Your rights? So, cheating to further your agenda, doesn't that mean denying the rights of others? And, would that be your definition of Socialist? You do realize that there are social democracies out there, which you erroneously-on-purpose call Socialist? You do realize that you willfully aided and abetted in high crimes and misdemeanors, yes? Was it worth it?" she spat.

"If I believed it was worth it, I wouldn't be here right now talking to you," he said with what sounded like genuine remorse in his voice.

She waved him off. "I hate you politicians who use whatever convenient fecking boogey man is in range, so you can scare people into getting your way, even if that includes treason or suborning treason. And now you've not only fecked yourself, you've helped feck the rest of us, too."

"I wish I could go back and change it," he said simply.

"My belief in your sincerity is the only reason I'm listening to you right now. How do I know I can trust you?"

"You don't. But let me remind you, by arranging this private meeting with you and the others, nothing benefits me. There is nothing stopping any of you from blowing me off and going right to the press with what I'm telling you."

"The press? The same press who bent over backwards to help Scholtz get elected? That press?" Maguire snorted, her cynicism crystal clear.

"I understand, Sergeant. There isn't anything you can say to me right now that I haven't already chastised myself

with, repeatedly."

Maguire studied him briefly. Segundo showed no signs of deceit. Either he was better than any liar she had ever encountered, or he was telling the truth. "If I agree to this, what happens next?" The glimmer of optimism in his expression didn't go unnoticed by her.

He let out a slow breath. "You will get orders that transfer you to a new training program. If anyone asks, it's a pilot program that will see whether cross training certain MOS's should be implemented across the board. Ultimately the program will 'fail.' Those in the program with you will all be there for the same purpose."

"Which is?"

"To stop whatever this plan is. If that can't be done, to prepare for it and then destroy them."

She smiled. "And what aren't you telling me. One of those things that you really should tell, but you don't think I'm going to like."

"How do you do that?"

"My mother was an O'Malley. That should tell you all you need to know."

He nodded his head. "Before we send you back to a regular unit, we'll have to use hypnosis to implant a chosen code word which will bring back memories we will have to suppress until you are needed."

"Wait...hypnosis? Yeah, you're right. I'm not liking that."

"It is only meant to save your life. You can go through our specialized training and when we are ready to hypnotize you and place you in your temporary assignment, if you don't agree with what we're doing, you can opt out. But if you do opt out, I cannot guarantee your safety."

"It doesn't sound to me as though you can guarantee anyone's safety at this point."

"Perhaps not, but you will be better equipped than most people to handle whatever comes."

Maguire stared at him blandly with all the confidence of someone who had no doubt in her own survival abilities.

Segundo nodded with a half-grin. "Okay, even more

equipped than you are now."

"Okay. Then what?"

"The intent is to activate the group before whatever this is can be set in motion."

"And if you can't?"

"I have a small circle who know what I know. If I am killed, the knowledge won't die with me. There will be someone to activate the team," he promised.

Maguire looked at him for several long moments. She'd already made her decision; she just wanted to watch him squirm a little. And he definitely registered on the squirm meter. This was not a man used to asking for things. "I'll give it a go," she said finally.

Maguire twitched, and opened her eyes, instantly awake.

"You okay?" Prescott whispered, shifting her gaze back to watching the area outside their camp.

Maguire blinked several times. "Yeah. Memories." She sighed out loud and crawled out of her sleeping bag. "You know, after passing the Fionaglagh course, all I wanted to do was emigrate back to Ireland and be a soldier for *her* for a change. Maybe I should have."

"What? And miss all of this?" Prescott's voice was laced with sarcasm. "We can't change the past, Maguire. Someone else was playing the tune."

Maguire nodded as she started shoving things into her rucksack. "Well, it wasn't the Star-Spangled Banner they were playing, now was it," she said with disgust.

"No, it wasn't."

***

Maguire and Prescott continued to journey northwest, staying aligned with the highway from Sanctuary to Lewiston. After crossing the bridge over the junction of the Clearwater and Snake Rivers into Washington state, they picked up State Road 12 at Clarkston and hiked west. They kept away from any main thoroughfares, though they did note that the roads they paralleled were in much better condition than those they had encountered on their trek to Idaho.

"Is it just me or have you noticed the more northwest we go, the less the world is destroyed?" Prescott asked as they began to ascend yet another peak.

Maguire stopped and stretched her back muscles. "A-firm. The air smells fresher, cleaner. Could be all the undamaged trees and vegetation that are clearing it up."

"I wonder why this area of the country was chosen to be spared and made the headquarters of all this insanity," Prescott mused.

"Hopefully Dr. Madras can shed some light on that." Maguire finished stretching and began walking again. "I'm wondering why a major access point to this state was not guarded and why we aren't seeing anyone patrolling the highways."

Prescott looked at her and nodded. "Maybe Dr. Madras can shed some light on *that*."

***

"You told Angel what?" Noble's voice rose with every word.

Anna remained calm. "I told her I would ask you, but we agreed that she has to straighten out her attitude first."

"You had no right to do that, Anna," Noble said stiffly.

"Why not? Until now, you had no idea why she was acting out. She doesn't see those boys the same way you do. They are her friends, and she misses them terribly. What harm can come from letting her see them and spend some time with them, especially if she never leaves my sight?"

"May I remind you that you were raped?" Noble shot back. "Do you honestly feel you could overpower two strapping teenage boys if they decided to take advantage of my granddaughter?"

"You will never need to remind me that I was raped," Anna said, her voice barely above a growl. "I live with those memories every damned day. Even given my own experience, I know that not every male who walks the face of the earth is a rapist. We could go to see the boys on the days their mother goes. Do you honestly believe they would do anything in front of their own mother?"

Noble crossed her arms. "Nothing would surprise me."

"Look, Angel is willing to become a productive member of your compound. She is eager to show you that she can earn your trust. And your love," Anna added.

Noble's hands dropped her to her sides. "My love? She thinks I don't love her? She is my life!"

"You're dealing with a hormonal teenage girl whose emotions are dramafied by puberty. Yes, she thinks you don't love her, and she also believes that you blame her for her mother's death."

Noble looked stricken as she slumped down into her desk chair. "She truly believes that?" At Anna's nod, Noble's bearing took on an air of defeat. "I...I've tried to be there for her. We were both thrust into a situation we didn't want. She wanted her mother, and I didn't want to have to raise another child. But I've always tried to be fair with her and—"

"And overbearingly cautious and protective?" Anna finished for her. "Angel needs physical affection, Rachel," Anna said gently. "She needs nurturing. She needs you to tell her that you love her and convince her that you mean it. I think you both have some growing to do with each other, but that's just my humble opinion. Maybe both of you need to start earning each other's trust. She's your granddaughter, not one of your troops. She needs her grandmother, not a drill sergeant. She's also making the transition from child to young lady, with the passions and instincts that go along with that. The question at hand is, if Angel stops behaving like a kid, will you stop treating her like one?"

Noble ran a hand through her hair. She stared at her desktop for a moment, then focused on Anna. "Wow. You may look timid, but you sure know how to cut right to the heart of something. Maybe I should have sent Angel to you when you first got here."

Maybe Jess would still be alive if you had, Anna thought. She chose not to express that sentiment. "Maybe we wouldn't have hit it off then. Why don't we just go from here and see what happens? You know, *you* could always accompany her to see her friends."

"As if she would want me along," Noble murmured.

"Who knows? Your relationship with her might have done a complete one-eighty by then. In the meantime, you have a young lady who feels very lost and detached. Don't leave her isolated. That will only make things worse, and you could end up with another tragedy on your hands."

Noble gripped the armrests of her chair, then relaxed and blew out a resigned breath as she looked up at Anna. "Thank you, Anna. You have done a great deal for me today, and I don't know if I will ever be able to properly thank you."

Anna smiled. "Let's see how it goes first. I'm not so naïve as to think she couldn't be playing us both. Teenagers are good at that. But I got the feeling she was sincere."

***

Maguire and Prescott checked their map and began walking adjacent to Highway 261 north, then west along 260 to Connell. As it started to rain heavily, they decided to take cover in what looked like an abandoned Burlington Northern Santa Fe Rail depot. As Prescott did her best to make their sleeping accommodations comfortable, Maguire checked out the entire building.

"Nothing here but dirt, dust, webs, and an overwhelming stink the closer you get to the restrooms," Maguire said. "Thankfully someone broke all the windows, so the smell isn't contained." She scanned Prescott's temporary set-up.

Prescott proudly gestured to the long benches she had turned into inviting albeit narrow cots. "What do you think?"

"I think you made them much too comfortable," Maguire said.

"And that's a problem?"

"Yes, because although this building seems long deserted, we still have to take shifts as lookout. Those benches look too warm and cozy to ever want to leave."

Prescott frowned. "Must you be so Mr. Spock about everything?"

Maguire shrugged. "Someone has to wear the pointy ears. I'll take first watch."

***

"Come on, Rachel, this is ridiculous," Carrie said in protest. "You know, you used to trust me until that loony toon, Maguire, came on board. I never thought you were that kind of friend."

Noble placed her pencil down on her desk, picked up a stack of papers and tapped their edges against the wooden top to even them up. She set them down and folded her hands on top of them. "Carrie, let's get one thing straight here." Noble looked up and locked onto Carrie's eyes. "We are not friends, we are survivors together. I do what is best for the safety and security of every woman in this sanctuary. I gave you responsibility because you led me to believe you could handle it, and I had my hands too full after the attack to monitor you. However, with the arrival of Maguire and the others, something changed in you. I—"

"That's not fair, Rachel. Everything was fine until they got here, and you know it. I haven't change, but it sure seems like you have," Carrie accused.

"The fact that you just admitted you haven't changed is what concerns me the most, Carrie," Noble's voice was not raised, but her tone left no doubt that this was not a friendly chat. "Have you always been a predator around the women here?"

"Predator?" Carrie's laugh was an indignant bark. "See, you're using Maguire's words. That's what I mean— suddenly, Maguire became your Holy Bible of reliability, and those of us who have been loyal to you are being dumped by the wayside."

Noble's eyes narrowed. "Are you serious, Carrie? Do you think this is the third grade here and every few days I have a new teacher's pet? Grow up! I am well aware that you despise Maguire. I have a hard time getting under that prickly exterior myself, but I understand her. She is a mission-first soldier, and everything else takes a back seat. She doesn't have time for the popularity game. She is who she is, and she is perfectly fine whether we like her or not. So, that said, when she came to me to discuss your predatory –and I am purposely using that word–behavior toward Anna, I was shocked, but I knew it had to be true because she is too focused on tasks to waste time making things up. Her telling me, and then Prescott and Anna backing it up, wasn't done to take you down or get you in trouble. Maguire wasn't going to stay anyway, so what purpose would that have accomplished?" Before Carrie could speak to that question, Noble held up her hand to stop her. "Carrie, you have a problem. I cannot abide predatory behavior here, and the gender of the predator matters not."

"Jesus, Rachel, they were lying. They told you I'm something I'm not."

Noble sighed. "You aren't helping your case any. I spoke with Anna, who has nothing to gain by telling me how you behaved toward her at least twice that she is willing to admit. We've already discussed Maguire, but Prescott also caught you trying to force your unsolicited affections on Anna. I've known Devon for many more years than I have known you, and she's not a Maguire fan, either, so it would make no sense for them to gang up on you."

"First, how do you know Anna didn't come on to me and then back out when her friends came along?"

"First, to my knowledge, Anna is straight, but even if she isn't, both Prescott and Maguire know her better than you do, and from their descriptions, Anna's body language indicated she was not interested. You should have backed off. One of the main reasons I started this sanctuary was so women wouldn't don't have to face the 'No means Yes' mindset of the patriarchy from which they escaped. Second, Lisa Jennings and Nelly Kim also met with me after they heard about your run-ins with Maguire and Prescott, and they told me you have been aggressive toward them, also. I won't have it, Carrie. I won't have the women here not feeling safe from one of their own."

"Jennings and Kim? God, I was just kidding around with

them. A little harmless flirting. I thought they could take a joke," Carrie said defensively.

Noble shook her head. "You know, Carrie, that's always one of the first things guilty men say when they get caught sexually harassing women. The thing is, if they had responded to your flirting, then it wouldn't have been a joke, would it?"

Carrie's face was red with exasperation at Noble clearly not buying her rationalization. "I can't believe you're doing this to me."

"You did this to yourself," Noble said. "You made these choices all on your own. Choices have either consequences or rewards. How this ends is up to you."

Carrie looked down at her feet, then back up at Noble. "So, what are you going to do with me?"

"I am removing you from your supervisory position. Until I come up with an appropriate disciplinary action, you will be confined to your quarters. I was going to restrict you to a monitored area of the silo, but you'd have too much access to the women who bunk and work down there. So, your cabin it is. You are not to leave it at all at night, and during the day there will be an escort at your door to take you where you need to go for specific necessities. Any variation from that will be reported to me. Any inkling of retaliation against Anna, Lisa, or Nelly, and you will have to find yourself a new place to live."

"What? You'd actually kick me out of here?" The shock was clear in Carrie's tone.

"If you don't police your own behavior and learn from this, you bet your ass I will."

"And how long will I be under house arrest?"

"That will depend on you, but it will be at least until I get a head's up from Dr. Madras about what the game plan is."

"But..."

Noble returned her attention to the file on her desk. "You're dismissed. Malcolm and Patnode will accompany you to your quarters." When Noble looked up, Carrie was still standing there, agape. "I said you're dismissed, Carrie." This time she didn't look away until Carrie spun on her heel and exited, followed by two women who looked like giants compared to their charge.

***

Anna was finishing her breakfast in the mess hall when Angel slid to a stop at the side of her table. She was carrying a bowl of cereal and an apple. For a moment Angel looked down at the floor, swallowed hard, then looked up and locked her gaze with Anna's.

"Can I sit with you?" Angels voice vibrated with uncertainty.

Anna experienced a momentary flashback. How many times in school had she asked that question, only to be laughed at while being rejected? She slid over on the bench seat. "Sure." A genuine smile ghosted over her lips as she looked at the concoction in the bowl while Angel took a seat. "You made jumble."

For a moment forgetting her fear, Angel smiled widely. "I loved jumble. All those different flavors, and the colors."

"My favorite was Cocoa Pebbles, Corn Pops, and Captain Crunch," Anna recalled.

Angel giggled. "Three C's. I liked the Raisin Bran, Lucky Charms, and Cookie Crisp combination myself. But here, since all we have is an overstock of stale Cornflakes, Cheerios, and Rice Krispies, I just pretend it's my favorite jumble." She pushed her spoon around her concoction. "What are you doing today?"

"Why do you ask?"

"I was kinda hoping to come along with you." Angel cast her eyes down to her breakfast, seemingly anticipating a 'No' in Anna's eyes.

Anna smiled as she leaned forward and gently touched Angel's arm. "I think we can make that happen."

Two hands slammed down on Anna's side of the table. Salt and pepper shakers, paper napkins, and dishes jumped in unison. Anna looked up into the beet red face of Jane Dettmer, Carrie's second-in-command of the Guard.

"I don't know how you did it, but Carrie is suspended and under house arrest. So, tell me what is so fucking special about you that my commander is now—"

Anna cut her off. "In trouble? How about because of her actions, not because of mine." Her voice was strong and even. "I did not ask for her undivided attention."

Dettmer straightened up. "She tells a different story. Everything was fine until you and that psycho, Maguire, got here."

Anna saw the anger radiating off Dettmer and tried not to show her nervousness, until she looked beyond Dettmer and saw Noble entering the mess hall.

Dettmer glanced over her shoulder to see what had caught Anna's attention. She backed away, pointing at Anna. "Don't think this is over," she said in a menacing tone.

When Dettmer was gone, Anna felt a tug on her sleeve. She looked over at Angel, whose eyes were impressively wide. "That was kind of scary. Do you want me to tell Gram?"

Anna shook her head. "No. Thank you, Angel, but your gram has enough on her plate right now, and that might only make things worse. Let's finish breakfast and get on with our day," she said with more confidence than she felt.

***

Individually, Maguire and Prescott had gotten possibly three hours of rest, some of it sleeping. It had been a little over thirty hours since they had left Sanctuary, and they were both feeling the fatigue.

Neither was traveling at the quick pace they had maintained the day before, and it seemed to take forever to hike the eighteen miles over harsh terrain from Connell to Othello. In reality, it took less than five hours. Had neither been in the physical condition they were, the trek would have taken much longer. At Othello, they moved south, parallel to State Route 24, taking stock of their increasingly woodsy surroundings. Their camouflage clothing was sure to keep them well concealed, in the event that they needed to be. So far, they had encountered no other life except for flora and minimal fauna.

When they were approximately twenty-eight miles into the current leg of their journey, they began to hear sounds that they hadn't heard in nearly a year: civilization. They slowed their pace and instantly went into stealth mode, following the path toward the noise.

"What the fuck?" Prescott whispered, as they moved into a thatch of trees surrounding a clearing.

"I don't know," Maguire answered. "The recon said nothing about troops being in…" she checked her map "…Basin City." She slunk to the ground and crawled up to the base of a large evergreen trunk.

Prescott moved up beside Maguire, her binoculars already out.

"Wow." Prescott's exclamation did not indicate the need for fight-or-flight mode. Her mouth was gaping open when she handed the field glasses to Maguire.

Maguire focused on the area Prescott had been viewing. There was no evidence of any military presence and the main street seemed to be bustling with normal small town activity, as though Armageddon had not occurred, or at least had not affected this piece of the country. She handed the binoculars back to Prescott. "What the fuck?"

"I know, right?" Prescott said. "I wonder if anyone has some real coffee."

"Yeah, probably not a good idea to ask. We don't know if they are supposed to alert anyone about strangers popping in."

Prescott let her head fall to the ground. "Gee, thanks again, Mr. Spock."

"Insufficient facts always invite danger," Maguire quoted.

"Jesus. You're a 'Trekkie'."

Maguire just grinned.

Chapter Seven

Noble watched as the militia went through their paces. Baumer had been adamant that the militia be taken off Sanctuary duties after their initial basic orientation, insisting that they not be considered a part-time unit but more like a standing army. That meant they had to perform normal patrol duties and continue training to keep their skills sharp. Noble watched the drills with a critical eye and was pleased that these women were obviously taking their responsibilities seriously.

Master Sergeant Mercedes Lewis stepped up beside Noble to observe the activities with her. "They're shaping up nicely, but their mettle won't really be tested until some kind of shit hits the fan." Lewis smiled easily to take the sting out of the observation.

Noble nodded. "They're not bad. How are we doing with alerts?"

"We've only had one since they finished training. It's mostly been patrols and setting perimeter stations that aren't obviously perimeter stations," Lewis reported.

Noble knew that Lewis hadn't wanted to get back into the military life full-time, yet desired to keep her skills and knowledge sharp, which was why she had agreed to move to Sanctuary when it was first started. After the world changed, there was no longer a choice. Lewis was new to her current position, but after fifteen years in the Army, Noble had no doubt that the sergeant knew what she was doing.

Noble did not take her eyes off the troops. "I'd like drills to happen. Random, unpredictable, even the middle of the night."

"Something I should know?" Lewis asked quietly.

"Unofficial for now. This might not be over, and I do not mean that in a good way." The answer was cryptic and clear at the same time. "How many of our residents live outside the silo, how many inside?"

Lewis blinked. "I can find out."

"By end of business today?"

"Yes, Ma'am." Lewis clearly recognized that as an order, no matter how it was posed. "Secondary billeting?"

"Contingency plans for that, and get them prepared for DEFCON levels," she finally answered. "I know I'm putting a lot on your shoulders…"

"Ma'am, my experience is in Admin and Logistics. In Korea, I breathed plan-and-delegate at brigade level. I have a good staff that knows what to do, including my civilians. Lieutenant Baumer was kind enough to let me pick and choose. You give me my parameters, we *will* make it happen." There was pride and stubbornness in the promise.

Noble allowed herself a smile. "You've seen professional armies. How do they…" she jutted her chin in the direction of the militia. "…rate?"

"Raw. But the potential is there. You've got good veterans as your training cadre, and the training outline Baumer and that lunatic came up with is intense. I wish *my* Basic had been as hard. There were things I definitely didn't get."

"Did we miss anything?" Noble asked in all sincerity.

Lewis thought for a long moment. "Let me ask the cadre and think a little on it. If we come up with anything, I'll let you know, Ma'am."

"Good enough." Noble smiled then. "And for the record, Master Sergeant, Prescott is a lunatic too."

Lewis grinned. "That's the lunatic I was talking about. I don't call Maguire a lunatic, Ma'am."

Noble was intrigued and just had to ask, "What do you call her?"

"Wraith."

"Wraith?" Noble was confused.

"Ma'am, all due respect, look up the definition of 'wraith', then go look for the unofficial, real record for the Korea action. There were some units we depended on to go beyond their official duties. Some were Special Forces, some were just normal units who got good at killing the enemy." She hesitated, then whispered, "Very good." She shook her head. "Maguire was in one of those units. They might have been trained as MPs, but they were damn good at more than traffic control points, because sometimes things go to hell in a hand basket."

Noble couldn't stifle her curiosity. "Are you speaking from personal experience?"

A shadow in her eyes, Lewis nodded slowly. "Not Maguire's unit, another one. You ever seen supply wonks killing the enemy fifteen feet away?"

"No."

"Once you have, you make it a point to listen to the radio transmissions when you're stuck in the TOC tent, and to read the after-action reports."

Lewis' tone was guttural, and as Noble turned and looked at her, she swallowed hard, seeming to push away the memories, at least for the moment. For some reason, "Nubian warrior" and "princess" both flitted through Noble's mind, and she shook her head slightly. "I thought I had the Korean files," she said to fill the silence.

Lewis' laugh came from deep in her throat. "You might have *some* of them, Ma'am. Check General Digmar's files and notes, if you have the authority, and the computer smarts."

The sly tone told Noble that Master Sergeant Lewis knew a great deal more than she had spoken about. Noble allowed a genuine grin. "I might have that ability."

Lewis began to move away. "Get his recipe for jungle juice, if you can. I know he wrote it down somewhere." She smiled as she moved out purposefully.

***

Maguire and Prescott had moved away from any obvious civilization, southwest toward the Columbia River. By the time they reached Ringold Springs, they were dragging. They continued along the edge of the water until they found the boat launch.

Prescott sat on a large rock to take a break. "Now where?"

Maguire pulled out the map and studied it. "Now we just need to find a usable craft to navigate the river from Ringold to the Vernita Bridge area, so that we can stay as close to our timeline as possible."

"Finally." Prescott took a couple swallows of water from her canteen and then pulled an energy bar out of her pocket. She removed the foil covering, pocketed the wrapper, then took a bite out of the bar. "Will we be able to get some real sleep tonight instead of crappy cat naps?"

"Doubtful. I wouldn't plan on any decent sleep until we get to Yakima. Maybe not even then."

"Great," Prescott muttered unenthusiastically.

***

Maguire took the lead as they followed along the riverbank, looking for a vessel that would transport them on the next stage of their journey. As if they needed any further complications, it began to rain.

After finding nothing but scrap, they eventually came upon a couple of boats that looked intact enough to still be floatable. One was so fancy, Prescott was almost salivating at the thought of spending the next few hours in dry luxury. When Maguire passed it by, Prescott called, "Wait, what about this one?"

Maguire pointed to the ground. "Fresh cigarette butts on the ground. Someone is keeping their eye on this one."

They walked a bit further in silence until they happened upon an eight-by-four-foot dinghy tied to a larger, half on land and half sunk boat. Maguire stopped in front of it, and Prescott began a close inspection.

"Oooh, it's one of those polyethylene, double hull thingies." Prescott noted Maguire's quizzical expression. "What? My father-in-law owned one a little bigger than this. That kind of hull is supposed to make it safer." Prescott stepped around the small craft. "This has obviously seen better days."

"Obviously," Maguire deadpanned. "Did you really use the technical term 'thingies'?

Prescott nodded with a full grin and began to walk away. "Good thing we don't have to use that one, though. I can't imagine having to spend a day or more freezing on something as compact and unprotected as that is." At Maguire's silence, Prescott turned and glared at her.

"What? It's perfect," Maguire insisted.

"No. No, Maguire, it's not perfect," Prescott said, incredulous. "This doesn't even qualify as horrible. It's barely big enough for one of us plus our packs, and there is no cover."

"Suck it up, buttercup. We need to be stealth, so we need to be small. We can't make a lot of noise, so we need something light that can glide pretty smoothly on the water. The colors are khaki and forest green, again perfect to stay close to the bank and go unnoticed. It has oars, as dilapidated as they are, to move us along when the current isn't working in our favor."

"It's pouring, it's freezing, and the closer we get to Yakima, the more likely it's going to be snowing. Is it too much to ask that we find something that has two berths inside or underneath?"

"Yes. Look around. We don't have time to shop around for the perfect accommodations. Hardly anything we've come across will even stay afloat. We're in a time crunch, and this will get us from point A to point B without us getting caught. That makes it our best option."

"But—"

"We slept and managed in harsher conditions for a lot longer than a day on our journey to Sanctuary."

"Can we at least tent our ponchos, maybe keep us a little less drenched?"

"Jesus, Mary, and Joseph, you've gotten soft," Maguire grumbled. "Being tented will filter out sounds and visuals, and that might make us vulnerable to attack or capture. In case you've missed the last couple of towns we passed, we're not in Kansas anymore. But we'll take shifts. Now help me turn this over to check for cracks and holes, and if it doesn't have any, help me drag this puppy away from the shore. Then you can burrow yourself into your poncho while I take first watch."

"Maguire! Do you really want to navigate miles of river in this?"

"Why not? The water is supposed to be pretty serene. It's not like we're on vacation, Prescott. Tie your ruck into the cleat on your side, and I'll tie mine over here."

Prescott grumbled and muttered the entire time they inspected the dinghy, tied in the rucks, and pulled the craft out to the water. Even though they were already drenched from the rain, immersing themselves in the river was still a shocking temperature change.

As soon as they were moving with the stream, both women climbed into the small vessel. Maguire sat on the small bench in the middle, between the sculls that were locked in place. Prescott sat on a molded-out seat area on the aft, so close to Maguire that their knees were touching.

"It's too small." Prescott removed one of her ponchos from her ruck and quickly wrapped herself in it.

"Get over it," Maguire said, surveying their surroundings. "If we catch the current, we should cut at least half a day off of our trip time."

"Fat lot of good that will do if we both die of pneumonia." Prescott sneezed, twice, as though emphasizing her point. She rubbed her nose on her wet jacket sleeve, glaring at Maguire the entire time.

"And when we reach our destination quicker than we planned," Maguire said, disengaging the oars, "you'll be thrilled." She started to row with even, powerful strokes. "Get some rest, Prescott. It'll be your watch soon."

"Oh, yeah, I'll get right on that," Prescott mumbled, starting to shiver.

CHAPTER EIGHT

A little over ninety minutes had passed when Prescott realized she was not going to get anything resembling rest. She took over navigating the dinghy's progress up the river, rowing almost leisurely while Maguire seemed to actually nap. She regarded Maguire with equal parts admiration and annoyance for being able to relax at all. Still, knowing Maguire, she was sure any semblance of chilling out was a façade.

The rain had tapered off to a drizzle, and the exercise of rowing was keeping Prescott's body temperature at a fairly comfortable level. They had not yet run into any activity or threat that had caused them to go on alert. Prescott had finally unclenched and calmed somewhat by the time the boat was passing a sign that told her they were approaching an area of the Hanford Reach called White Bluffs. It was now on the darker side of dusk. The current propelled them forward at a nice pace, and Prescott placed the oars back into their locked position while she monitored the quick, steady flow. If the rest of the trip on the river was like this, she knew it would be a piece of cake.

Even as she was thinking that, something jolted the dinghy slightly sideways and, before Prescott could react, the small boat lifted a bit then splashed back down. "Maguire?"

Maguire was instantly alert. "What was that?"

"You tell me, O' Sergeant MapQuest," Prescott answered, looking around them to find the source of the turbulence. "Shit. We're going faster."

"Huh. Maybe we are hitting a rapids," Maguire commented.

"Rapids?" Prescott almost shrieked. "You didn't say anything about rapids!" They hit another small whitecap that made Prescott's belly flip. The boat landed back down in the water and then dipped into what felt like a hole that battered them with a rough spray from all sides. After a few subsequent minutes of surreal stillness, Prescott said, "That wasn't so ba—"

Another big drop sent them both airborne, but before they could be ejected, the craft rose up to meet them and their behinds slammed into the boat with such force, it felt as if it would crack every tooth in Prescott's head. Before they could recover their balance from that jolt, the dinghy flowed into an eddy line and sent them spinning. Prescott hung onto the tiny bench, while Maguire lunged forward and grabbed the oars.

The vessel straightened, and Prescott got her bearings. She wiped water out of her eyes and glared at Maguire, who was holding the oars in position, ready to steer the boat when she could.

"What the fuck, Maguire?"

Maguire shrugged and stayed vigilant. "Wasn't on the map."

The dinghy surged through a gorge without any upset. As they sailed around a large rock, there was a thunderous sound downstream.

"What's that noise?" Prescott asked. She didn't need an answer; she instinctively knew their wild ride was not over. The closer they moved to the ominous rumbling, the more it went from sounding like thunder to sounding like a freight train coming at them at full speed. "Maguire…"

"I know."

Abruptly, the craft dropped a couple of meters, then a few feet more, taking on enough water to sink it, but just as quickly as it filled, it emptied. Maguire was somehow still at the helm, while Prescott had her arms locked together around a tiny, unoccupied section of the middle seat, hanging on for dear life. Prescott knew that no matter how many layers of clothing she had on, her body would be one big walking bruise if they survived this pounding.

Again the section of the river became deceptively calm, but this time Prescott did not buy into the illusion. She relaxed her grip only slightly as she looked up at Maguire. The rigid posture and the grim expression on her colleague's face were not encouraging. The nature of the stream swiftly changed again, and Maguire steered the small boat over the countercurrent, was forced into a whiplash swivel and, when they leveled out, hit a series of severe ripples. That last challenge was so harsh that the dinghy reared up and balanced on its nose before it crashed back into the water, upside down.

Prescott was thrown with frightening velocity into the Columbia River. When she surfaced, she was coughing water out of her burning lungs and gasping for air as she looked around for Maguire. Her eyes locked onto the bobbing hull of the empty dinghy. "MAGUIRE!" she hollered.

The roar of the rapids seemed to be lessening as Prescott and the capsized dinghy floated into calmer waters.

"Maguire!" Prescott yelled again. She was trying not to panic, but the relative stillness did not bode well for Maguire's survival. She was about to call out Maguire's name again when she heard a splash.

"Woo hoo!" Maguire's voice echoed off the walls of the ravine. "What a feckin' ride!" Then there was silence.

Prescott swam in a circle until she saw Maguire's head pop up out of the water near the stern of the dinghy, so she sluggishly swam to the boat, treading water when she reached Maguire. "What happened to being stealth?" Prescott growled.

"That was awesome!" Maguire gushed, working to right the dinghy.

"Awesome?" Prescott spat. "*Awesome?* I almost drowned, you maniac! Let me tell you something, I just survived what felt like an 85 mile-an-hour douche. I thought you were dead. Awesome, my ass!"

"Come on. Stop bitching and help me turn this thing over. If we are feckin' lucky, our packs are still cleated in. There's a boat launch by the Vernita Bridge. We could lay in there."

When the craft was operable again and they had clambered back in, Prescott glowered at the beaming Maguire, who was literally bouncing up and down on her seat. When Maguire finally realized Prescott was staring daggers at her, she said, "Oh, come on. That was–"

"One more word and I swear to all that is holy, I will cut you."

***

Several more hours of rushing along with the continuingly strong current finally placed them just beyond an old boat launch on a washboard rough, dirt road, near a cluster of dry, heat-baked shrub. They pulled the small craft over to what appeared to have been a slate and stone wall, now fallen and half scattered.

They hid the dingy under a rock shelf, piling driftwood and rocks around it to complete the camouflage. With the boat secured, Maguire and Prescott shadowed the main road to Yakima. They started to see hotels and restaurants and other signs of activity, but not knowing who was friend or foe, they kept to their plan and stayed hidden.

With no words exchanged, Maguire and Prescott pressed on, deliberately walking on rock until they entered the woods. Once they were deep enough to not be seen from the shoreline, Maguire halted and pulled the waterproof map from inside her coat. They squatted and leaned their heads together, then Maguire pulled off her glove and traced a finger along a line on the map.

"We're here. The coordinates we have to get to are here." She pointed to a small grease pencil circle. "Twenty-five miles and fifteen hundred feet in not easy elevation." Her expression was disgruntled.

Prescott eyed the map. "Jesus. Twenty-five miles in a day? Can we do that in a day?"

"If we press hard, we could, possibly. Not sure about the mountain travelling," Maguire admitted. "Final ruck for MP School was twelve miles. We did it in eight hours with twenty-pound rucks. Final ruck for Irish Ranger Wing was forty miles, with sixty-five pounds in our rucks. We had to do it in ten hours. My feet were feckin' hamburger. I'm not going to lie to you, this is going to suck. The bright side is that we're only carrying about twenty-five pounds. Your choice—fast or slow?"

"So, let's go fast. If we see anyone, we evade."

Maguire smiled. "Just what I was thinking. Eat and drink on the move." She gazed at the sky. "I don't know whether to wish for the snow to come in or to wait."

"So, either way, this is going to suck."

Maguire chuckled. "There you go looking on the bright side again."

***

Anna approached the compound's exterior hygiene area where the showers were located. The structure was a wooden lean-to, with ten individual stalls separated by wooden doors. The open area faced a section of the west wall to give the impression that there was some semblance of privacy. Each enclosure had its own watering can, suspended by a hook, and line that ran from the ceiling to the reserve tank that held river water, heated by solar energy. Each woman, before taking her shower, would fill the bucket, rehang it, and use the string to tip out water and then return the container to upright, only using the amount within the bucket to bathe. It was primitive, but it worked, and it saved a trek into the silo where the lines were usually long. The interior hygiene area was where most of the children showered, as they seemed to be more bashful about the sanitation issue.

Anna secured her stall, prepared her bucket, and disrobed, hanging her clothes on the peg outside the door so they would not get wet. She placed her towel over her clothes and tipped the can. While she showered, she let her thoughts drift to Maguire and Prescott. She hoped they were okay, would do what needed doing and hurry back. Now that Carrie had been dealt with, she didn't feel unsafe, although Dettmer's playground bully act had been a little disconcerting. At least she knew Maguire and Prescott were, and would always be, there for her. But she had not really clicked with anyone else, and she was lonely.

When her limited water supply ran out, Anna squeezed the excess water out of her hair, then reached over and grabbed the towel. She dried off, then set the linen aside to wrap around her hair after she was dressed. As she took her clothes into a dryer area of the enclosure, she heard raised voices and some commotion. She ignored it.

Dressed, she stepped out of the stall, stopping when she heard someone calling her name. Looking in the direction of the voice, her heart started pounding when she locked eyes with Carrie. Although the two women guarding her were at her side, they apparently were not going to keep Carrie from verbally interacting with her.

Clearly having no modesty issues whatsoever, Carrie began to get naked outside the stall. "I owe you one, Anna," Carrie said, goading her. "Your bodyguards can't help you now. You fucked me over with Noble. That's not something I'm likely to forget." She stepped into the enclosure and turned to face Anna. "And don't go running to Noble. I'll deny it, and so will they." Carried nodded her head toward the guards, Patnode and Malcolm.

Anna noted the reaction of Carrie's minders, who found a sudden interest in any direction other than Anna's. Not responding to the baiting, Anna turned and walked away. Given the level of pettiness being demonstrated, she felt as if she was back in Junior High, not in an environment where the occupants were preparing for world war shit to hit the fan. She needed to find Lisa Jennings.

CHAPTER NINE

The Yakima Training Center sat on three thousand acres on the outskirts of the city of Yakima, Washington. Located nine miles north of the city, 164 miles southwest of Joint Base Lewis McChord, it was nestled northwest of the Columbia River, on the eastern slopes of the Cascade Mountains. Once Maguire and Prescott had stealthy maneuvered around the military installation without being detected, they would have another forty miles, as the crow flies, to get to Cle Elum Lake where, hopefully, Dr. Madras was still safely holed up in her vacation cabin.

Maguire and Prescott had stopped to get a read of their surroundings. They were at a higher elevation now and were shocked to find there was still no snow. Maguire took a small, makeshift periscope from her backpack and set the tube to peek above the crag. The more mountainous topography reminded her of sections of Afghanistan, with its surrounding landscape of extensive smooth hollows divided by intruding furrows. Coated with sagebrush, volcanic outcroppings, arid ravines, and large rock formations situated in the high desert, the stark and hostile terrain seemed the perfect area for multiple training exercises and operations.

"You know, I had a woobie sewn into my coat and I'm still freezing my ass off," Prescott said, breaking the silence. Maguire gave her an odd look, and Prescott returned, "What?"

"You just said woobie."

"Yes."

Maguire was perplexed. "Not an expression I thought I'd ever hear from your mouth."

Prescott snorted. "I've said a lot of things in my lifetime.

I even went to a tea party with my daughter." Maguire was still staring. "Now what?"

Maguire shook her head slightly. "Just trying to reconcile that visual with your behavior towards Anna on the trip."

Prescott was silent for a few moments before she locked eyes with Maguire. "I had a subset of orders from Nobel. If we picked up stragglers, I was to push their buttons and push hard on their weaknesses."

"To what end?"

"You really have to ask? Only as strong as the weakest link. Sound familiar?" Prescott let out a long breath. "I pushed Anna hard, and she took it until she got sick of it." She chuckled. "Did she tell you about letting me know we might be entering bear country and asking if I wanted to take point?"

"She did not." Maguire's amazement was clear in her voice.

"She did," Prescott affirmed. "The actual truth, Maguire, is that I'm not always an asshole, but sometimes I have to be. And yes, there are also times I hate your guts and would very much like to kill you. Just something to think about."

"So noted. And that goes both ways." Maguire went back to watching through the periscope as Prescott leaned against a wall of rock. From their vantage point, Maguire saw nothing she deemed unusual. She took the periscope down and mumbled, "I could use a hot meal and a hot shower."

"You?" Prescott chuckled. "The consummate grunt wishing for creature comforts?"

Maguire's eyes became slits. "You smell like rotten salmon, and that's after river baths. I'm going to guess that I smell the same or worse. So, yes, a hot shower with soap would be a good thing. For both of us."

Prescott lifted her arms to sniff her pits. "I don't smell anything."

"Then your nasal passages have been severely compromised because let me tell you, if a grizzly bear happened upon us right now, he'd think he'd died and found an upstream utopia." Maguire put up the periscope again, shifting its focus.

"Hey, super soldier! You could always kill the grizzly and get us some red meat, you know! Not my fault we've had all surf and no turf!"

"Maybe I should get Anna to point one out." Maguire chuckled and lifted the periscope up again.

"Still a lot of nothing out there?"

"Just the peaceful outer east perimeter of the training center." Maguire was silent for several moments. "Noble said this rocket scientist is needing rescue, right?"

"Satellite engineer," Prescott grumbled. "Yeah. Her message indicated she needs us to get her out. Why?"

"Too bad she wasn't right here. There doesn't seem to be any guard activity. Since I've been watching, there have been no perimeter checks, no movement, no signs of any life. It's like they have no fear that anyone is alive to confront or attack them. We could just walk right in, grab her and go."

"That sounds like a trap," Prescott said.

"Maybe." Maguire pondered the possibilities. "But maybe they really are that smug. I would guess they know that there are random bands of survivors, but they probably believe they've pretty much killed off all factions that could challenge them militarily. At least for a while."

"Makes sense. Still, that gate could be protected by cameras," Prescott suggested.

"It could. Doesn't make a difference if the cameras aren't closely monitored." Maguire pulled the periscope back down. "Not that it matters at this point. We just need to stay low, get to the Yakima River, and follow it northwest to Cle Elum."

"Another wild rapids ride?" Prescott asked warily.

"No, too easy to be spotted now. We walk the rest of the way."

"Thank God," Prescott said gratefully.

Maguire stowed the periscope in her ruck. "Ready?"

Prescott took in a deep breath of cold, fresh, mountain air, then blew it out. "I'm glad we are finally on the last leg. At least it hasn't—" Just as she was about to spit out the word "snowed," a fluffy white flake landed on her eyelash. Another hit her nose, followed by a sudden squall. "Son-of-a-bitch!"

***

Anna was standing in the doorway of the makeshift dojo where Jennings had just finished a workout. Jennings was always sincerely friendly and approachable, so she took a deep breath and then called out, "Hey, Lisa, got a minute?"

"Sure. What's up, Anna?" She wiped perspiration off her forehead with the sleeve of her sweatshirt.

Anna looked around. "You alone?"

"For a minute or two. Something on your mind?"

Anna stepped into the room and walked over to Jennings. "How much do you trust Malcolm and Patnode?"

"I have never seen anything from either of them that would make me question their loyalty to Noble."

"What about their loyalty to Carrie?"

Jennings appeared to be mulling over Anna's question. "I don't know. Why do you ask?"

"You know Rachel assigned them to guard Carrie, right?" When Jennings nodded, Anna continued. "This morning when I was coming out of the shower, Carrie was about four stalls away. She was just getting in." Anna then told Jennings what had followed.

"And Malcolm and Patnode just stood there and let her?" Jennings sounded incredulous.

Anna nodded. "They did nothing to shut her up or take her out."

"That's not right." Jennings wiped her face with her sleeve again. "Have you said anything to Noble?"

"No, not yet. But Angel was with me when Dettmer kind of threatened me, so I have no doubt it will get back to her."

"Dettmer, too?" Jennings sighed. "I guess I shouldn't be surprised. Carrie and Jane have been fuck buddies for a while."

"Oh, that's a lovely visual." Anna made a face. "Dettmer's warning and those two letting her talk trash is one thing. Hopefully Dettmer was all bluster, and my escort will draw the line if Carrie insists on getting physical. Can I get you to refresh me on some defensive moves, just in case?"

"Absolutely. Would it be okay if I mention something to either Malcolm or Patnode? I could tell them I overheard Carrie this morning and I was wondering why they didn't say anything to her. Maybe believing there was at least one other witness, especially someone who has also reported Carrie's previous behavior, they will keep a tighter rein on her."

"That might be a good idea," Anna agreed. "What about Dettmer?"

Jennings hesitated. "Jane can be a nasty piece of work when she's got a wild hair up her ass. Maybe if I talk to the other two, they can say something to back her off."

"Thank you, Lisa. It's worth a shot. I'm going to town in a few days to talk to Doc about moving in with him, so how about I come by early tomorrow before I go talk to Rachel about leaving?"

"You're leaving the compound? Damn! Is it because of Carrie?"

"Not really. I mean, it expedited my decision, but I want to apprentice with Doc anyway, and it will be easier if I'm right there." She hoped she wasn't jumping the gun, because she didn't yet know for certain that Doc wouldn't mind.

"I understand. I'll try to catch Patnode or Malcolm sometime after they lock Carrie in tonight. And why don't I meet you here at first light to review some tactics?"

"Works for me. Thank you, Lisa."

***

Prescott crankily trudged behind Maguire through a rapidly building snowstorm, cursing with pretty much every step. The precipitation was sticking to the ground and had accumulated to a little over a foot, covering the landscape with a thick, heavy, wet, white layer, making the traveling slower and more treacherous.

"Should've kept your mouth shut, jinx," Maguire yelled back over her shoulder.

"It doesn't help that we're walking along the riverbank,

you know. Just makes it colder. I'm starting to lose feeling in my feet," Prescott griped loudly.

"Then we should walk faster," Maguire suggested, picking up her pace.

Prescott hurried to catch up with her. "What's our ETA? Any idea?"

"When we reach Ellensburg, we'll be more than halfway. That should be in about two more hours. Then we need to find where the Cle Elum River forks from the Yakima and follow that to Cle Elum Lake. Once we are at the lake, we locate the cabin, scope it out and get in, then grab the package and get out."

"Is there any possible way we can take a break to warm up and get some rest while we're there?"

"That will depend on the circumstances when we get there."

"My boogers have frozen inside my nose, Maguire," Prescott groused.

"Your *boogers*?" Maguire shook her head. "How old are you? Five?"

"How would you describe it then?" Prescott challenged.

"I would say that proboscis matter has fastened itself to the fine hair-like fibers in my nasal passage and has solidified."

Prescott glared at her for a moment. "Yeah, whatever. Anyway, I hate that. Tell me you don't hate that." She was peeved by Maguire's neutral expression. "Doesn't anything affect you? Excessive heat, torrential rain, arctic cold, blizzard?"

"It *all* bothers me, Prescott. I just don't whine about it like a little bitch."

"Fuck you, Maguire," Prescott said with lackluster indignation.

"No. You have frozen boogers. That's just icky."

"Wait...are you saying you'd fuck me if I didn't have frozen boogers?" Prescott tone was both horrified and curious.

"No, because you'd still be you, and that's just icky," Maguire said without looking back.

CHAPTER TEN

By the time Maguire and Prescott reached the lake, it had finally stopped snowing. It took them another fifteen minutes to locate the refuge of one Dr. Elaine Madras, if the provided coordinates were correct. They hid in a thicket of snow-covered forest across from the cabin to surveil the layout and assess the situation before making a move.

Maguire had foolishly assumed the term "vacation cabin" was code for an out-of-the way, barely accommodating shelter. The structure was actually a picturesque, A-frame log cabin surrounded by fir and spruce trees and covered in a blanket of white. It looked like a Thomas Kinkade painting come off of the canvas. All of the large windows on the front of the chalet had a dark finish that Maguire guessed was most likely to keep out the cold in winter and the heat in the summer. She hoped they would also be bulletproof, or at least bullet resistant, but that might be hoping for too much. Who—other than she —would build a vacation retreat and make it into a fortress?

"Not exactly what I was expecting," Prescott stated for the both of them. "Unless the inside is totally opposite the outside, or she's being kept in a storage space, it doesn't look like this cabin would be too hard to get used to. Are you sure this is the place?"

"We checked the longitude and latitude points at least five times. These are the coordinates Madras gave Noble. We are where we're supposed to be." A hint of suspicion crawled into Maguire's tone. "Though nothing on the exterior appears to indicate a dire situation." She pointed to the freshly fallen snow around them. "No sign of any activity at all. This snow is untouched. No human tracks, and no forest dwellers' tracks, either."

"Forest dwellers? Who are you looking for—Bambi and Thumper? Look at the weather. No one in their right mind would be out in this." She stared hard at Maguire. "And I mean no one."

"Something's not right. I can feel it."

"You thinking it's a trap?" Prescott stared toward the cabin.

"Honestly? No. It doesn't feel like anything leading to an ambush because the little hairs on the back of my neck aren't standing up."

"Jesus," Prescott barked, "how would you know in this weather?"

"Trust me, I'd know. Something is off. I'm not sure what, but no time like the present to find out." Maguire stood up and ran across the small distance between their stakeout spot and the darker side of the cabin.

Prescott joined her a few seconds later. "Fuck, Maguire," she whispered harshly, "give me a heads up next time, will ya?"

"Not my problem you don't pay attention." Maguire squatted down and got her bearings. She let her eyes adapt to the lack of moonlight, as the trees they were now under were too thick to allow much illumination. Once her eyes had adjusted, she spotted a full trashcan and a woodpile. A majority of the small logs were covered with a dense coating of snow, but there was one area that had only a light dusting of snow, where logs had apparently been recently removed from the stack. Maguire's gaze swept to the back of the cabin, locating a door. Boot prints that tracked back and forth from the stack of firewood to the two steps told Maguire that this door was a main access and egress point. She moved again, toward the cabin, this time with Prescott hot on her heels.

"Is that door alarmed?" Prescott pointed to a keypad by the doorframe.

Maguire studied it. "No. It's a magnetically coded lock. It's specifically made to look like an alarm system, but it isn't one."

"How can you tell?" Prescott whispered.

Maguire dug into one of the utility pockets in her jacket. "First, only an idiot would put an alarm on the *outside* of a door or window. Second, I can tell by the way it looks that it is not electronically connected. Third, we used to have locks just like this in the bunker where the LT and I worked." She continued to search through additional compartments of her uniform. When she found what she was looking for, she held it up for Prescott to see. "And fourth, when I was a kid in Ireland, some of my mother's family were, shall we say, *outside* the law. Not that I'd have any personal knowledge of their activities."

Prescott didn't quite manage to keep her sarcasm in check. "You know, you barely sounded convincing. Keep practicing." She glanced at the object in Maguire's hand. "A keychain? What's that for? There's no way you have a key to this door."

"That's correct, but I have the next best thing." She held up the unexceptional small, gray fob. "This is a demagnetizer, kind of like a skeleton key. It's an older model, but it should work."

Prescott obediently followed Maguire to the door, then watched as Maguire held the implement between her thumb and forefinger and lined it up with the lock. Seconds later, the door clicked.

Prescott goggled. "How—"

"It neutralizes the pin and the poles and gives the impression that the properly teethed key was inserted." Maguire repouched the tool.

"And you just happened to have one on you?"

Maguire raised an eyebrow. "It's one of those things that once you have them and see their convenience, you never let them go. You know, like a P-38 or a handcuff key." She reached to the back of her uniform and took out her Sig Sauer, then put her finger to her lips and slowly nudged the door open.

Prescott removed her Glock from its exterior leg holster and followed Maguire inside.

***

Maguire and Prescott moved stealthily through the luxurious log cabin, silently checking every room for risk. Not only were all the rooms empty of any human presence or visible electronic surveillance, there was Christmas music playing at a low volume from an iPod hooked into a speaker over the fireplace. Embers were fading in the firebox, and the faint odor of wood smoke lingered in the air. Maguire and Prescott exchanged glances. Nothing looked or felt out of the ordinary. Which was not at all what they had expected with a "rescue."

Maguire signaled to Prescott to follow her into what seemed to be the master bedroom. After discerning there was no immediate threat, Maguire concentrated on the single lump in the queen-sized bed as she approached the still figure with caution.

The person was cocooned in a comforter and snoring lightly. Maguire looked at Prescott, who shrugged, then nodded and aimed her Glock at the center mass of the supine form. Maguire reached over and shook the sleeper's shoulder, then coiled back, ready to spring instantly if things turned hostile.

Their captive blinked several times and slowly lifted her hands from beneath the blankets to show they were empty. Maguire gestured with the barrel of her pistol for the occupant to get out of bed, keeping her covered with the weapon as the woman complied and then pointed to her robe.

Prescott walked over to the garment and searched it. Finding it clear of any weapons, she tossed it to the woman, who put on the robe then whispered, "Office."

Maguire nodded, and gestured for the person she hoped was Madras to lead the way. They followed quietly, and once in the office, the woman turned on the light.

The occupant of the cabin was a sturdy woman of medium height with long, curly, mahogany-colored hair and eyes so dark they were nearly black. But the flash of fire in those eyes belied her calm demeanor as she walked into the room and sat down. They watched as she activated her notebook computer and tapped out a sequence of letters and numbers. She monitored the screen until it rang out a tone.

Madras looked directly at Maguire. "Staff Sergeant Maguire, I've read your file. Oddly, breaking and entering was not one of the skills listed." Her voice was smooth despite the situation.

Maguire studied the woman briefly before she spoke. "You have that advantage over me. I know nothing about you except—" She stopped abruptly and looked cautiously around the room.

"I'm Doctor Elaine McCloud Madras. No one is listening. Every two or three days I change the code and adjust the algorithms to ensure we can stay undetected."

"How can you get away with that? You're so close to JBLM and Yakima, I would think they would be keeping their all-knowing eye on everybody they could," Maguire said.

"They trust me."

"If they trust you, why do you require rescuing," Prescott asked. "Why can't you just walk away and disappear?"

The dark eyes pivoted their attention from Maguire to engage Prescott. "And you are?"

"Devon Prescott."

Madras nodded. "Actually, I don't need rescuing. I need to stay here to monitor the nuthouse. I just had to get the sergeant here to come to me so that I could give her the information she needs to help get our world back."

Maguire bristled. "I don't like being lied to."

"It wasn't an egregious lie. The world needs rescuing, and I am one of the few who hold the key."

"Maybe you need to get to the point. I don't like games," Maguire said tersely.

"Agreed. I don't like them either." Doctor Madras took a deep breath. "So, in the interest of the truth, I have to say that there's no way I'm going to have this conversation with the two of you smelling the way you do. You can take turns in the shower while I make coffee and breakfast. After that, we can go over all of this." With that, she turned on her heel and walked out of the office.

For a long minute, neither woman spoke, then Prescott said, "Well, that was rude."

Maguire glared at her, then rolled her eyes and shook her head as she left the room.

Prescott shrugged. "Guess we do smell."

***

Anna, sweating and nearly out of breath, mentally reviewed how she had once again ended up flat on her back on the mat. It wasn't that she couldn't perfectly execute the unarmed self-defense move as instructed, but in the face of an attack, she was thinking about what she had to do instead of just doing it. The maneuver involved immediate, instinctive counter-action and leverage rather than brute strength, but she just couldn't seem to overcome hesitating before reacting, so every time, Jennings had pinned her. Even with all that Anna had been through, fighting had not become second nature to her. That had to change, because Maguire was right—she had to take back her own power. Anna growled in frustration, and Jennings relaxed her grip.

"No worries, Anna. It just takes practice. The ability is there, you just have to keep at it or, as you've seen this morning, you lose the advantage over your attacker." Jennings remained straddling her. "Since you're already on the floor, let's work on another technique. Most fights usually end up on the ground, so it's good to learn how to fight from the ground. Do you remember any of these moves from class?"

Anna searched her memory and found that she did recall a few maneuvers. "Which one is this?"

"Getting out of a mounted choke hold," Jennings supplied. "Let's try it. And don't think, just react." She suddenly leaned forward and put her hands around Anna's throat.

Suddenly the tactic flooded back to Anna like a dam breaking. She had made it a point to remember this one maneuver out of all of them, because this was the position she had been in when she was raped for the first time. Her right hand enclosed around Jennings' right wrist and her left hand grabbed behind Jennings' right elbow, deadlocking Jennings' arm to her chest. Anna's left foot hooked around Jennings' right foot, trapping Jennings' leg, and then she lifted her hips and rolled the instructor over so that Anna was now on top, freeing her hands so she could strike blows to Jennings throat, nose, or eyes. It happened so fast that it took them both a few seconds to register that Anna had completed the maneuver.

"Anna! That was awesome! If you can do that one like that, you can do all of them like that."

Anna grinned triumphantly at the praise, pumping her fist into the air while she excitedly bounced up and down on what she had temporarily forgotten was Jennings' stomach. "Yes! Can we do that again?"

"No," Jennings rasped as she stilled Anna's hips.

"No? But you just said—"

"I mean, yes, we can do it again, but please leave out the part where your butt is smacking against my belly, or my breakfast is going to be all over the front of you."

***

Following prolonged hot showers, Maguire and Prescott returned to the kitchen, reinvigorated and wide awake as adrenaline erased some of their exhaustion. Madras had built up the fire, and a fresh pot of coffee sat warming for them on the counter.

"Are you sure you don't want to get some sleep before we start?" Madras asked, bringing mugs of coffee as they each took a seat. She gestured toward containers of cream and sugar already on the table.

"Not me," Maguire said. "I can sleep later. I'm ready to get this show on the road."

"I'm not sure I'm as dedicated as that, but I will go for as long as I can. What's for breakfast?" Prescott asked.

"What would you like? I don't have access to a lot of variety, but I'm sure we can come up with something filling."

"Pizza," Maguire said. "I haven't had a pizza in so long."

"Oooh, pizza. That sounds good to me, too," Prescott agreed.

"Pizza?" Madras shrugged. "Sure. I have pepperoni and pepperoni."

"I'll take pepperoni, then," Prescott said. Maguire nodded.

"It's frozen, but it's gourmet. Is that okay?"

"It's pizza," Maguire said. "I'd let it thaw in my mouth at this point."

"Thank you," Prescott called after Madras as she left the room. She was much more relaxed, but Maguire's stiff posture indicated that she had yet to let her guard down.

Madras reentered carrying a round baking stone and a frozen pizza. "As I said, it's not fresh, but cooking it on this over the fire will make it taste homemade. Pizza used to be my go-to breakfast after a long night. It makes life seem almost normal. Believe me, that doesn't happen often around here."

Maguire took a sip of her coffee. "What is normal around here?"

"Insanity," Madras answered succinctly. "That's one of the reasons I needed you to come here, to this place. The other reason is that we must agree on a plan. I can communicate with Nobel on occasion, but it's not something that can happen on a regular basis. I'm inside the circle, but there's no telling how long that will last."

"How did that happen? Scholtz is not exactly woman's best friend," Maguire observed.

"I'm special, Sergeant. Two years into his first term, I'm the whiz kid scientist who turned in her parents for being in the country illegally," she admitted quietly. "They were deported."

"Do you know where they are now?" Prescott asked.

Madras closed her eyes. "They're almost certainly dead."

"How could you do that?" Maguire's accusatory tone made no effort to spare the woman's feelings.

Madras appeared unaffected by Maguire's condemnation. "We needed someone to do it. I was the only one who could. My parents understood that. They volunteered. In truth, my parents were here legally. They agreed to the charade so that I could become the golden girl of the party."

"And it doesn't hurt that you have the whole package going, right? Brains, easy on the eyes, and not overtly pushy for a woman," Prescott observed. "Very good planning."

"Segundo is a smart man," Madras answered simply. "My parents trusted him implicitly."

"Where is he?" Maguire poured more coffee into her mug.

Madras let out a shaky breath. "I don't know. We were supposed to make contact after the *government* regrouped. There are a few others who are missing as well. No one has admitted any knowledge of what became of them. All I can do is to carry on as we planned."

Chapter Eleven

Doc was bringing in an armful of wood from the covered cord of wood piled at the side of the house, when he saw a horse trotting up the road to his fence. Recognizing Anna, he quickly detoured from his front stoop to greet her. He smiled broadly as she dismounted, tethered her horse to the fence, and moved easily into his arm for a side hug.

Anna took a step back and looked up at him. "Hi, Doc," she said warmly.

"Anna! It's great to see you. What brings you to my door? Are you sick? Everything okay at the compound? Is it Maguire and Prescott? Have you heard from them?"

Anna grinned. "Slow down, Doc. One question at a time."

She followed him inside, where he set the wood down by the fireplace, then returned to the kitchen and put the kettle to boil.

"Tea?" he asked.

"That would be lovely." She watched as he fetched the teabags and two mugs. "So, I'm not sick, everything is okay at the compound, and Maguire and Prescott should have made it to Washington by this morning. I'm sure Noble will hear something today."

"Ah. Good. So, what brings you into town?"

"Are you still willing to let me apprentice with you?"

Doc stopped and turned to face her. "You want to do that?"

"Yes, I do."

"I thought maybe you had found a new calling when you settled into the compound."

"No. And I really haven't settled in, especially since Jess

died and both Maguire and Prescott are gone. I mean, I've made some friends and I have learned a lot, especially about defending myself, but…" Anna sighed and pushed a strand of hair behind her ear, "I just feel, I don't know, unfulfilled. And, like I don't belong there. I think I belong here."

"You said everything was okay out there, but it seems as if you're holding something back." Doc pulled out a chair at the table and gestured for her to sit, which she did. He sat opposite her. "What's really going on?"

"I don't know." Anna shrugged. "I just miss everybody, I guess. Most of the women are nice, but I don't feel a connection with them like I do for our little group. I know it might sound weird, but I feel safer here with you."

"Has someone there made you feel unsafe?" Doc asked gently.

"I had a couple of run-ins with Carrie that have not been fun. I thought it might get really bad once Prescott left with Maguire, but Noble has put Carrie under house arrest and I have to believe that's enough to keep her away from me. It's not that, Doc. I just feel out of place. I've shadowed the healers, but it seems like they just tolerate my questions, that I'm really just a big pain. You never acted like that."

The teakettle began to whistle, and Doc got up to remove it from the heat and pour water into their cups. "I would love to continue to mentor you. It's a long way to come in every day, though. Not sure I feel okay with you doing all that traveling back and forth alone. I mean, everything seems fine right now, but we never know when the shit might hit the fan, especially given what Maguire has remembered."

"Doesn't this place have three bedrooms?" Anna said quietly.

Doc set the steaming mug down in front of her. "Yes. One is mine and one I use for a personal office, but there is another bedroom I'm not using." He raised an eyebrow as he looked at her searchingly. "Did you want to come live here?"

"If that wouldn't be any trouble, yes, I would." When he didn't respond right away, Anna said, "If you have started to, maybe, see someone and you think it would be inappropriate,

I understand. I just thought that if I am to be your assistant, it would be easier on both of us if I lived right here." She blushed. "Presumptuous of me, I know."

"No, not at all, Anna." Doc sat down. "I would love to have you here, and it would be easier on both of us. I could use the company, too. I am not seeing anyone. I don't think I'm ready for that yet even though it's been nearly a year since my fiancé Amy died, and despite the fact that it feels as if Mr. and Mrs. Cameron have paraded every eligible woman left in Idaho through here," he said with an easy smile. "When do you want to move in?"

***

"How did they do it?" Prescott asked Madras as Maguire bit off a mouthful of pizza, only to have the melted cheese stretch out, break off, and flap against her chin. When she yelped at the heat of the stringy mozzarella, Prescott smiled. "That's gonna leave a mark." She returned her attention to Madras. "How did they catch us all so unawares?

"It was pretty simple, actually," Madras answered. "Scholtz was placed in the presidency, as you know, despite the outcry over the sham of an election. The Scholtz administration began to censor the press, then pick and choose outlets that would advance their agenda of evoking fear. Soon the only news we were getting came from the biased sources. The networks essentially became State TV."

"I remember, before that, corporations and sponsors started losing a lot of money," Maguire said, wiping her mouth with a napkin.

"Yes. Which is why they all started jumping on board with Scholtz's gaslighting. After all, they helped him into the highest office in the country by giving him carte blanche publicity and never calling him on any of his campaign lies." Madras took a sip of her coffee. "The new government had the media exactly where they wanted them, so they fed them propaganda."

"And the press swallowed every morsel tossed to them, didn't they?" Prescott commented.

"Yes, they did." Madras continued. "They fabricated several stories about terrorists obtaining highly-enriched uranium and making improvised nuclear devices. All the while they were planning the launching of a full-scale attack and building up their own facilities so that they and theirs would survive the devastation. They didn't want a nuclear winter because they wanted to be able to establish their new world order in their lifetime, so they used limited nukes and other weapons of mass destruction that would do the job but not make specific regions of the earth uninhabitable for them."

"How did they do that so effectively?" Prescott asked.

"It's easy when you brainwash enough people willing to do your bidding because the reward is, well, a consecrated promise," Madras said.

"You mean they used Rapturists to fulfill an 'End Times' prophesy," Maguire stated flatly.

"A gold star for Sergeant Maguire." Madras glanced at her computer screen, then looked back at her guests. "Just like radical jihadists volunteer to be suicide bombers because they get rewarded in heaven, that's what they did here. The Rapturists provided volunteers willing to sacrifice themselves to bring on Armageddon, and for that, they would be rewarded in heaven."

"But how did they get onto military installations?" Prescott asked.

"Because they had Rapturist jihadists implanted in different areas and ranks at each facility," Maguire said.

"Another gold star for Sergeant Maguire. At home and abroad. Most important was abroad. They needed to take out key points—Germany, Israel, Korea, England, and China," Madras took another sip. "Several Rapturists drove vans or trucks loaded with destruction into the heart of many major cities, and then detonated them. In a quarter of a second, the devices incinerated anywhere from five to ten thousand people, depending on the density of the area at the time. After about fifteen seconds, the death toll was 30,000 or more. Area casualties surpassed 100,000 after just twenty-four hours."

Madras took a deep breath and continued.

"Structures within a three to five-mile radius of the blast site were severely damaged if not completely demolished, and the contaminated area was estimated to cover 3,000 square miles or more. Some damage was even worse because of environmental factors such as topography and atmospheric conditions," Madras said, reciting planning statistics she had seen. "Other areas were hit with Electromagnetic Pulses, which damaged many, if not all, power grids, communication systems, and electronic devices in the affected areas. They were smart, though. They took the nuclear plants and *certain* energy grids off line just before it hit the fan. Those they can bring back up when the time is right."

"Everything happened quickly and without even a hint of warning," Prescott said, shaking her head.

Madras nodded. "Exactly how they planned it."

"Not exactly without warning," Maguire interjected.

"Well, yeah. I mean, everybody saw that the country was spiraling downward, but I think, we all thought something or some*one* would stop it," Prescott said.

"Someone did try," Madras reminded them. "Why Segundo couldn't activate the team before the destruction took place is something we can only guess at."

There was a thoughtful moment of silence, and then Prescott said, "Jesus! Why couldn't they see it was like two people pointing a loaded, cocked gun at each other? One shoots, the other will shoot in reflex. No one wins."

"Except someone did win. The results of their mutual annihilation game were well calculated." Maguire looked over at Madras. "So why headquarter here?"

"What's the first rule of hazmat training? Upwind, uphill, upstream. That's where we are. That's where they built their survival areas, and that's what was taken into consideration when the areas of detonation were selected." She took a deep breath. "But before the day of commencement, almost all strategic personnel were evacuated and replaced with selected leaders and soldiers from all over the world, as well as from military academies which have been secretly receiving religious indoctrination along with their military training over the past several years."

"So, let me take an educated guess," Maguire said. "They did a pre-emptive strike to kill off major populations in Africa so they could also harvest the resources without competition. China, like locusts, would come here and bleed us of any remaining resources we had, so they had to be taken out too. And, Korea, well, I'm thinking that something massive detonated at Camp Humphreys, big enough to take out the entire peninsula." She held up her hand as Dr. Madras started to speak. "I know, I know. Another gold star for me."

"What's the deal with the only effort to stop this insanity being training a group of selected people and then hiding them?" Prescott asked.

Madras smiled. "Mr. Segundo, in case you didn't know, was over a quarter Rappahannock. That tribe settled in Virginia years before it was a commonwealth. I am one-quarter Nisqually."

"Wait, I thought your parents were Eastern Indian," Prescott said.

"My mother came to the U.S. as a student and fell in love with a boy who was half Cherokee. She was pregnant with me when she was summoned back to India, where her parents paid an enormous amount of money to marry her off and cover her shame. She and her new husband moved back to the States when he was offered a prestigious job with the government. The man who raised me was a proud, traditional Eastern Indian man, and he took great pleasure in throwing my Cherokee heritage in my face every time he got drunk. Despite that, he was also a man who objected to what he saw the leadership in Washington doing to his adopted home. Even though he was a complicated man, I will always respect his sacrifice," Madras told her. "When I was old enough, I took a year off from school and embarked on a quest to find out all I could about my birth father and his bloodline."

"Did you get to meet him?" Maguire asked.

"No. Unfortunately he died a few years after I was born. I did get to meet my grandmother, though. That was an amazing, enlightening experience. I learned so much."

Madras drew an audible breath and expelled it slowly. "Anyway, every one of the people hand-selected to rise and fight this post-Apocalyptic battle has at least one-quarter traceable Native American blood running through their veins. Segundo said the white men have continuously raped our Mother Earth and nearly decimated the ancestry. He wanted the Nations to band together to take the country back, to rebuild it and be the governing body of the country."

CHAPTER TWELVE

After Madras' final declaration, Prescott switched from coffee to a full tumbler of the scotch from a bottle on the kitchen counter. When she resettled at the table, she stared at Maguire. "Did you know about this?"

"Not officially, but it didn't take a genius to see that there were a lot of native nations represented during training," she answered slowly, then sighed. "I don't decide policy, I just fight the feckin' wars."

"Are you telling me that we are actually going to have a long overdue, honest-to-goodness uprising to re-form this country?" Before either Madras or Maguire could respond, Prescott held her glass in the air and said, "I'm in." The contents of the tumbler were gone in two swallows. As she set her empty glass on the table, a frown appeared on her face. "But, as far as I know, I have no trace of Native American blood in me. I can still be in, right?"

Maguire snorted. "You don't have to be Native American to fight in the Resistance, goofball. You're already in it. The Native American element will be the leadership." She looked to Madras for confirmation, and then smiled when the doctor nodded. "Yep, I'm just racking up the gold stars today."

***

Anna knocked on Noble's open door and waited to be advised to enter. At "Come in," she stepped into the office and walked over to Noble's desk.

"Good morning, Anna. What can I do for you?" Noble asked pleasantly. She extended her arm toward a chair, inviting Anna to sit.

Instead, Anna rested her elbows on the back of the chair. "I came to tell you that I'm leaving."

Noble was obviously startled by Anna's announcement. "Leaving? Where are you going?"

"I will be moving into town with Doc."

"Oh." She looked at Anna curiously. "I thought with the Carrie issue taken care of, everything was okay for you here."

Anna had decided not to tell her about the most recent threat, and it appeared that Angel hadn't said anything either. "It's been fine. It's not you, Rachel. You've done everything you can to make me feel welcome, and Carrie is not your fault." So far neither Carrie nor any of her minions had caused any more trouble. Since she was leaving anyway, Anna had chosen to set aside any misgivings she still had. She had relayed the one-sided conversation to Lisa Jennings, and she knew Jennings would be looking out for herself and the others on Anna's behalf.

"I am thankful that you brought the issue to my attention. This is my compound, so it really is my responsibility to be certain that everyone feels safe. So, if it's not Carrie, then what? Not Angel?" Before Anna could respond, a look of comprehension washed over Noble's face. "Oh. Are you and the doctor…?"

Anna waited for Noble to finish her question, but then realized what Noble was insinuating. "Involved? No, we're just good friends. I feel comfortable with Doc. And he's going to let me apprentice to him. It will make me feel much more useful. And that way, if you occasionally need another healer here, once I'm trained, I can help with that, too."

"But I thought you were shadowing Noreen to learn those skills."

"I was, but Noreen and the others really don't seem to be in the frame of mind to have me hanging around them, much less teaching me anything."

"I could speak to them if—"

"No, there's no need. I don't think it is anything personal. They have their hands full, so my endless questions probably get under their skin. It probably would me, too, if I were them. Doc started training me during our journey here, and I really learned a lot from him already. I would like to build on that foundation, plus we have an easy rapport."

"Of course," Noble said. "You will be moving to town, then?"

"Yes. Doc has an extra bedroom, so I can stay right there with him. I'll leave in few days, after I make sure I've finished everything I promised to do." She took a deep breath before continuing. "I'd still like to work with Angel, if that's okay with you. The Camerons have a horse they've given to Doc, and he said I can borrow her anytime."

Noble smiled. "You have no idea how much I'd appreciate that." She took a breath. "Well, it's settled then, though I'm sorry to see you leave Sanctuary. You've been a breath of fresh air since your arrival, Anna, and you've really made a difference with Angel. You will always be welcomed back, anytime." Noble stood up and reached across the desk to shake Anna's hand. "Good luck to you. Is there anything from here that you would like to take with you?"

"Just a few personal items and some necessities for hygiene. Mostly I'm taking what I arrived with. Jennings could take me back to town on her next wagon trip, if that's all right with you."

"I'd like to send you with a radio, solar charger, and an extra battery. That's non-negotiable, by the way. Just in case. If there is anything we can do to get you settled, don't hesitate to ask." Noble walked her to the doorway. "I have to ask, are you sure this isn't about Carrie?"

"Positive." Anna smiled. "This is about me. Thank you for everything, Rachel."

***

"Explain to me what happened to prevent COG protocols from being implemented if everyone believes the US leadership is dead and gone," Prescott asked. "Because I always thought there was a Continuity of Government plan in place that lined up a sort of…replacement administration that would keep the country from being without a leader. Yet no orders have gone out, no one has stepped up to take charge. It's been over nine months since the devastation, and what's left of the country, and the world, is still in complete chaos."

"Ah, but it isn't," Dr. Madras said. "Because the people in power knew they would survive, and everyone imperative to their plan was moved to safety before the attacks began. There was no need for a COG because the same people are still running the show. Right now, the strategists are mapping out the logistics for the reclamation to start slowly moving east and south to claim territories and rebuild."

Maguire mulled that over for a moment. "They can do that now, can't they?" She looked out the kitchen window where the afternoon sun, muted by tinted glass, was casting a sepia tone over the access road to the lake. She returned her gaze to Madras. "They were clever about manipulating which areas of the country would be uninhabitable and which would just be temporarily affected."

"Indeed," Madras agreed. "In your cross-country trek to Noble's compound, did you notice that on every destroyed military installation you happened upon, all of the confinement facilities were intact?"

Maguire thought back to when she and Baumer had spent the night in one at Fort Bliss. "I know Bliss' stockade was in pretty good shape. In fact, come to think of it, it almost looked reinforced."

"It was. In areas designated to withstand the attack, people on the inside ordered the posts and bases and camps to fortify their jails. Underground data centers, like the one you were in, Maguire, will also be stripped of any technology that might have outside or satellite connectivity, and then will be utilized in the reorganization."

"As what?" Prescott asked.

"Confinement," Maguire answered. "They'll round up dissidents and anyone else who disagrees with the Triumvirate." She didn't look at Madras for confirmation; it just made sense. "Shades of feckin' Stalin and Hitler. Pick your feckin' despot."

"Holy shit!" Prescott looked to Madras. "What about other upwind, uphill, upstream locations? Sure, northwest

Washington state is their HQ, but there have to be other planned areas of survival."

"More than you might think," Madras said. "That reminds me. You'll need to go to Cheyenne Mountain."

"What? I thought Cheyenne Mountain closed," Prescott said.

Madras made a sound that was caught somewhere between a chuckle and a cough "Oh, no. NORAD and USNORTHCOM moved to Peterson Air Force Base in '06, but the Mountain was still active as an alternate command center."

"If it is still manned, why would we want to go there? I know you think we're good, but we can't break into a facility that is a mile inside the mountain and protected by two 23-ton blast doors. And if it is electronically monitored, we sure as hell aren't going to sneak up on anyone inside," Maguire said.

"You don't have to. When everything went down, there was only a skeleton crew of one hundred and twenty-two on duty. Seven of them are ours. One of those seven is a very talented hacker. Unbeknownst to NORAD, USNORTHCOM, and the Triumvirate, we control Cheyenne Mountain."

"How the hell can you do that?" Prescott asked.

"I told you, we have a hacker. And the six others who are there are programmers, communications officers, and one head of security. As long as the other defense command centers believe that the Mountain is still a backup resource being kept safe by their people, they'll stay away. At least until they need it to start moving their operations eastward in Phase Three of their master plan. By then, we will hopefully be fully in place and ready for them."

"How the hell did we do that?" Prescott asked.

"All a part of Segundo's strategy," Madras replied.

"So, seven are ours. What about the other one hundred and fifteen? Don't they suspect anything?" Maguire asked.

"They believe everything they are told by Mountain SecCom. I mean, why shouldn't they? They have no reason to suspect anything in the world outside is any different from the information disseminated to them, right?"

"What are they being told?" Maguire asked.

"That conditions outside are still toxic and uninhabitable. Our hacker, Jermaine, makes sure that the images on the monitors and exterior surveillance cameras show a hostile and deadly environment."

"Jesus." Prescott ran her hand through her hair. "I know that the Mountain was designed to withstand a nuclear blast, but how did it survive an EMP?"

"The area was designed with structures deep inside a mountain of granite. Also, Navy-grade steel was used in the construction of the buildings—"

"Which would reflect the pulses and shield the equipment inside," Maguire finished, the lessons she'd learned during her year of training filtering into her brain.

"Right. So, operations were never affected," Madras added.

Maguire and Prescott both took a moment to absorb and process the information.

"What were the responsibilities of the skeleton crew? I'm guessing not all were system engineers, analysts, techs, or anyone that held anything higher than an active security clearance," Prescott observed.

"Varied. There are a few with those jobs, but because the Mountain was locked down at the end of a graveyard shift on a weekend, the personnel were mostly what you would expect to hold down a facility that only retained 8% of its original workforce to keep a back-up, mission support unit there."

"What are those inside telling the Triumvirate, NORAD, and the others?" Maguire asked.

"They are informing them that everything is going as planned, that all scheduled operations are on track and ready when they are," Madras said.

"And their Intelligence operations are stupid enough not to have checks and balances on that?" Prescott wondered out loud.

"Not stupid," Madras corrected, "arrogant. Stupid is the *last* thing they are, but they are chock full of hubris and believe they have pulled off the perfect world-wide coup. They don't even consider that there might be any traitors in their ranks, because who would *dare* defy them."

"Okay, so NORAD and USNORTHCOM stood down while Cheyenne Mountain was spoofed?" Maguire asked.

"They had their own mission and issues to worry about, and as far as they knew, the Mountain was secure and a secondary concern," Madras answered. "Look, Cheyenne Mountain as it was in *draw down* is so back burner to these people right now, it might as well not even be on the map." She exhaled a tired breath.

"How is Peterson being fooled? Surely a complex so huge that it works in conjunction with the underground operations at Denver Airport isn't taking the hacker's word that everything is fine at Cheyenne? You can't tell me that in over eight months, they haven't sent someone out to do an inspection," Maguire said.

"Actually, I can. Since most headquartered operations moved to JBLM, Peterson is also manned by a standby skeleton crew. They pretty much destroyed the entire planet, so they don't believe they have anything to fear from any external forces. What they did to the USA is temporary and was done in such a way that it can be repaired to suit their needs and their timetable." Madras grimaced. "You will, however, have to find three of our..." She thought for a moment. "For lack of a better term, we'll just call them gray hat contractors. They're assisting. That's as much as I can give you right now."

"Where are we marching off to next?" Maguire grumbled.

"After you return to Sanctuary and regroup, you will be going to the Lehi, Utah area. And no, I don't have an exact location." The expression on Madras' face did not change. "I'm hoping they're just not safe enough right now to contact us and will when they can. If and when that happens, I will get a flash message to you with grid coordinates," she promised.

"And what about me?" Prescott asked.

"That will be up to Maguire. Once you leave here, you will be equipped with all the information I have for your sector. Maguire will be in charge. All decisions and strategies from now on will be hers and those of whichever of the other leaders she decides to align with."

Prescott's lip curled. "So…she'll be my boss?"

"If you want to stay in familiar territory with your troops, yes," Madras confirmed.

Prescott sighed. "Well…shit."

CHAPTER THIRTEEN

There was a knock on the door of Anna's cabin before she heard the door squeak open.

"Anna?"

"Yes?" Anna walked out of the small kitchen and saw Angel peering inside. "Hey, kiddo. What's up? Isn't it almost curfew?"

"Getting there. Can I come in?"

"Sure."

Angel stepped inside and closed the door behind her. "It's cold out there. I saw the smoke from your wood stove, so I figured you were still up."

"I just poured myself some tea. Want some?"

"Gross, no. I hate tea."

"Afraid tea, water, or coffee is all I have to offer."

"Coffee?" Angel said with a sly smile.

"No." Anna smiled back at Angel. "You wouldn't get to sleep for hours, and your grandmother would kill me."

Angel clasped her hands behind her back and twisted side to side in nervousness. "Do you think maybe I could spend the night?"

Anna blinked, then brought the cup to her lips and blew on the hot tea, buying some time while she considered her response. "Why? Everything okay with your grandma? What's going on?"

"Nothing, but…" Angel's face fell into a pout. "You're leaving in a couple days, and I'm not going to get to see you much, and I'm gonna miss you and, well, you're much more fun to be around than Gram. I thought maybe we could have a slumber party."

"A slumber party?" Anna repeated. "Have you ever been

to a slumber party?"

"No. I've never had real friends before, other than Dylan and Shaun, and you know I would never be allowed a sleepover with them."

"Not at this age, anyway," Anna said. "Tell you what, kiddo. Square it with your grandma. If she says it's okay, how about tomorrow night? I can get everything I need done by then, and then we can have a slumber party."

"Awesome!" Angel bounded over to Anna and wrapped her in a hug. "Thank you, Anna."

Nearly spilling her tea, she held her arm out so that the hot liquid wouldn't slosh on Angel. "It's not a done deal yet, so…"

Angel released her. "I know, but I bet if I can't persuade Gram, you can."

"I'll stop by later and see what she's said. Is there anyone you would like to invite? Anyone your age."

"No. Remember, I told you, none of those girls like me."

Anna turned Angel around and gently pushed her toward the door. "You need to get home before you get grounded and then there's no chance for a slumber party."

"I know, I know."

Anna stood at the door and watched Angel run in the direction of Noble's headquarters. She grinned, shaking her head as she shut the door. "Oh boy."

***

The sun had set over the tree line in front of the lodge. The day had slipped by quickly, which was normal for winter, but neither Maguire nor Prescott had slept yet, and it hadn't registered how much time had passed until they realized it was dark outside.

"How did they convince Petrushev to abandon Russia for the US?" Prescott asked.

"I'm not entirely sure Russia has been abandoned, but that's just a guess. We have no evidence at this time to say there is any activity there, but he is too smart to not still have functioning resources there. I'm thinking that he prepared his country the same way we prepared ours. Scholtz is too self-absorbed and dictatorial to think anyone would betray him. From what we have gathered, Petrushev has convinced Scholtz that he brought Russia to us, at least his most elite cabinet, top fighting forces, and essential military stock," Madras explained.

Prescott shook her head. "Again, how could that happen right under our noses?"

"You really need to ask that after what they have already achieved?" Madras' tone was both incredulous and annoyed.

"Hey," Prescott barked, "you can drop the attitude. We're the ones who haven't had any sleep. If anyone gets to be impatient and cranky, it's us." She looked from Madras to Maguire.

Maguire quirked an eyebrow at Prescott and then fastened her stare on Madras. "She's right. We're allowed to ask questions, even if they're rhetorical."

Madras bowed her head, then glanced back up at them. "I apologize. It's just that I have so little time to bring you up to speed."

"Maybe we should call it a night then," Prescott said. "Start fresh in the morning."

"Agreed." Maguire stood. "I want to be able to retain as much as possible."

As though she had just remembered something extremely urgent, Prescott sat up sharply and looked at Madras. "Before we go to bed, I have to ask the most important question of all."

Madras sighed. "What could be more important than everything we have just talked about?"

"Do they still track Santa Claus on Christmas Eve?" Prescott asked with a straight face.

"I forgot about Santa Claus," Maguire said, her tone sad.

"How could you forget about Santa? Think of the children," Prescott lamented.

"And Rudolph," Maguire added.

Madras folded her arms and shook her head. "I swear you two are insane."

"For the record," Prescott stood up and pushed her chair in, "she's insane, I'm just along for the ride."

***

By the time Maguire arose in the morning, Madras was already up and about, puttering around in the kitchen. The aroma of brewing coffee welcomed Maguire as she stood in the doorway and stretched.

"Good morning, Sergeant," Madras greeted pleasantly.

"Is this routine for you? To be wide awake and functional at—" Maguire glanced at her watch, "—04:30?"

"Not usually. But as I said last night, we have a lot to cover. What about you? Normal wake-up time?"

"No." Maguire reached for one of the coffee mugs that had been set out on the counter. "I overslept."

That prompted a chuckle from Madras. "Right. How long before we should get your buddy up?"

"I'll give her another half-hour. She hasn't had a lot of sleep, especially in any comfort or warmth, for the past several days."

"Aw, you do care about her," Madras teased.

"Of course I care about her. I even respect her. I just don't like her. Generally."

Approximately thirty minutes later, Prescott awakened to an aroma that quickly drew her into alertness. She opened her eyes to see Maguire standing next to her bed, waving a plate back and forth in front of her.

"What the fuck, Maguire? I haven't slept this good in… Is that bacon?"

Maguire grinned. "It is."

"Real, honest-to-goodness bacon? Like from a real pig?"

"Yep." Maguire started to back out of the room, holding the plate in front of her.

As if in a trance, Prescott threw the covers back, exited the bed, and followed Maguire to the kitchen without further comment.

***

Anna had risen early, as she had much to get done before her departure from Sanctuary. She'd worked up a decent appetite sparring with Jennings, and since she had cleaned out all her breakfast food products in preparation for her departure, she decided to grab some fruit or cereal in the communal dining area.

She was halfway finished with a bowl of oatmeal when she glanced up and saw Dettmer heading her way. *Jesus, if this is going to be a daily occurrence, I'm glad I'm getting out of here.* At least, now that the self-defense training was coming back to her, she didn't feel quite so vulnerable, but she hoped she'd never have to use it. If all Dettmer was going to do was threaten her, she could put up with another day of that.

Then something surprising happened. Dettmer's path was blocked by Angel. Dettmer tried to push by her, but Angel stood her ground.

"Out of my way, little Noble," Dettmer snarled.

"No. Anna got your message yesterday," she said, just a hint of tremor in her voice. Her expression remained fiercely stubborn. "Back off, or I'll tell *big* Noble."

Dettmer smirked. "So, you're a little snitch." She tilted her head toward Anna. "Just like your tail-teasing buddy."

Angel hauled off and kicked Dettmer in the shin, which caused the woman to grab her leg and hop around howling. "Don't talk about her like that! And it's not being a snitch when you're doing the right thing against evil bitches."

Dettmer limped toward her menacingly. "Why, you little—"

"Problem here?"

Dettmer stopped and turned to see one of the tougher armed commando members behind her. "Yes, Noble's fucking brat—"

"I wasn't asking you," the woman interrupted.

Carol Quarterman was one of those people who was not to be messed with. She took her new military-type job quite seriously and, as Anna had noted, was devoted to Maguire. It had not started out that way, however. In the beginning of the training, she'd had a bad habit of rolling her eyes at Mags and Prescott in synchrony, which earned her the nickname Cyclops. After her attitude gained her what Maguire called "shit jobs," she focused, trained hard, and earned Maguire's approval as one of her best students.

"No. No problem, Cy." Dettmer raised her hands defensively and began to back away. "Just a disagreement." She looked at Angel. "Right?"

When Angel didn't answer right away, Dettmer started to fidget, and Anna couldn't stifle a grin.

Finally Angel looked up at Cy. "Yeah. We're good." She glanced at Dettmer. "For now."

"You done with breakfast, Dettmer?" Cy asked.

"I was just about to—"

"Get it to *go*," Cy ordered.

"Sure. Sure, Cy. It might be a while, there's a line." Dettmer's tone and demeanor were now yielding, her former bravado having completely disappeared.

"I'll wait," Cy said.

Dettmer nodded and limped over to the queue.

Angel walked briskly to where Anna was sitting and flopped down on the chair next to hers. "I almost peed my pants," Angel confessed.

Anna put an arm around Angel's shoulder and gave the teen a squeeze. "You were very brave. Thank you." She released her grip. "But, Angel, you have to be careful. I'm leaving here, you aren't. You don't want to get on their bad side."

"I think I'm already there," Angel admitted. "Thank God that Amazon butted in. I think Dettmer might have really hurt me."

"I wouldn't have let that happen," Anna reassured her. "I don't think anyone in here would have let that happen."

"Because of Gram?"

"Well, maybe before today. I think you may have just taken a step toward being your own woman today, my friend," Anna said.

"Really?" Angel asked, basking in Anna's praise.

"Really," Anna confirmed.

Chapter Fourteen

"What about the towns from here to JBLM?" Prescott asked. "They can't all be Triumvirate supporters." She had just finished a long, leisurely breakfast and was now doing the dishes.

"It doesn't matter," Madras said. "Wherever there is a population, there is now martial law."

"We saw no evidence of that, or of any military presence at all, when we crossed the state line and passed through Othello, not even in Basin City."

"Yeah," Prescott said, "And Basin City was populated. It looked as though nothing had happened."

"Basin City is a Rapturist outpost. They don't need an official military presence. They are militia with a full arsenal. They are *believers*. Did they see you?"

"No, we stayed hidden," Prescott said.

"Good. They would have shot you on sight. That's their standing order for all strangers."

Maguire glanced over at Prescott. "Good thing you didn't go ask for that cup of coffee you were hankering for."

"Did you see anyone or anything else on your way here?" Madras asked.

Maguire considered their trek. "No one appeared to be monitoring the Columbia River in the Hanford Reach from the hatchery to the bridge, but then, we tried to stay stealth."

"Stealth? *Stealth?*" Prescott barked. "Sorry to break it to you, Maguire, but your bonsai 'woo hoo' at the end our little rapids adventure was anything but stealth."

"Neither was you shrieking my name so loudly that it echoed off the ravine walls," Maguire shot back.

"I thought you were dead," Prescott muttered.

Maguire raised an eyebrow. "Wishful thinking, but, no."

Madras shook her head as she looked from one to the other. "Are you sure you two aren't in a relationship?"

Maguire and Prescott stared at each other with equal disdain, until Prescott said, "Not only no, but *hell* no. Why would you even ask that?"

"Because you fight like an old married couple."

Maguire and Prescott simultaneously each took a step away from the other, and Prescott wiped her hands on the towel before resuming her seat at the table.

"Maguire did notice that Yakima didn't appear to be too concerned about guarding their access points," Prescott said.

"I found that extremely odd," Maguire said, then added, "Arrogance again?"

Madras appeared to mull over the question. "Possibly. If they believe all their outlying areas are being guarded and they, at present, feel no threat from anyone, maybe they have gotten a little lax with physical security. All access points are heavily monitored, though. Or they're supposed to be."

"So, the military or militias currently control all areas, or soon will," Maguire noted.

"Yes, but not your *regular* military. Civilian authority has been suspended indefinitely, probably forever if they have their way, and the imposition of Rapturist military authority is now the law."

"Wait, so the crazy cultists are now our police, our courts, and our legislature? Doesn't martial law have to have some high ranking military member presiding?" Prescott asked. "Not that it probably makes any difference now, but Scholtz never served a day in the military and neither did Franklin."

"Not that I'm looking for another gold star, but something tells me that under the new rules, Russian President and former General Petrushev is now that high ranking military member." She didn't have to look up at Madras for confirmation that she had that answer correct. "If he follows his old protocol, he'll have a governor or a commissar. Can you find out who he and *they* might be?"

Madras eyes narrowed. "What are you thinking?"

Maguire's smile reminded Prescott of a grinning skull. "Hit list. Know who they are, and take them out hard when the time comes. I know it might be beyond your capabilities, but anything you can get us… It will be effective if *our* side takes them out, right?"

"Indeed," Madras agreed.

"What about long-term consequences? Aren't they concerned about that?" Prescott asked. "I mean we may be talking *decades* after the initial event—cancers, radiation poisoning, contamination…"

"They seem to have a solution for all of that," Madras said. "I have not yet been able to decipher what that is, unless they start something innovative like terraforming. My guess is that the affected areas are not a priority at this time, but will eventually be colonized."

"And I bet that the worst offenders and anyone resisting their new world order will be used do the rebuilding. That way, if the workers die from any kind of exposure, they can just be replaced with another dispensable body," Maguire surmised. She looked up to see both women staring at her. "What? That's what I would do if the situations were reversed. I'd use the people I considered enemies as guinea pigs to test the environment."

"But how can they believe they're going to have enough prisoners? How many do they think survived?" Prescott asked.

"It doesn't matter. Seems to me, a regime such as Scholtz, Petrushev, and Franklin want to enact will make prisoners as needed," Maguire said. "The closer we got to the outskirts of the Yakima center, the more life seemed to be going on as usual. I'm sure it's even more populated the closer one gets to Sea-Tac. I'm also going to guess that the surviving population in and around the Sound are clueless about what their immediate future holds, thinking that martial law is just for maintaining temporary order."

"Yes. That is how it will work. In the meantime, they will start indoctrinating children, creating more children conditioned to the ways of the new world order." Madras paused. "And they will focus on ethnic cleansing, so that eventually it will be a pure white race again. Except for the prisoners. They will need what they consider lesser races to do whatever they feel is beneath them, so there will also be mandatory procreation in confinement."

"Chilling, though nothing coming from that bunch would surprise me. Let's get back to the long-term consequences for a minute. What about the financial cost of the decontamination? My recollection of studies on that subject is that we would be talking about several areas of thousands of square miles of land. Everything on it would need to be demolished and hauled away to a containment location, and the toxic sites would have to be completely decontaminated before being useful again, in any manner. That would take years, maybe even generations," Prescott said.

"They don't care about cost. They have everything they need at their fingertips. They have the materials, the ways and means, and the workforce. They don't have to pay anybody for anything because they own and control everything," Madras said.

"But—"

"No, Ms. Prescott, you're thinking about the world we left behind, not the world we have now. Forget yesterday and start thinking *Dark Ages,*" Madras said. "You're thinking in terms of money. There is no money anymore. It's useless. It cannot buy anything. We now live in a world of bartering and power. There is no universal internet. There are no banks or financial institutions. They're all gone. Savings, stocks, bonds, annuities, bitcoin…none of that has value."

"Meaning," Maguire surmised, "you learn to trade what you have for what you need."

"Right." Madras nodded. "The rule of quid pro quo, except the lower rungs of the ladder don't get to name the barter. They get to trade their bodies and their bodies' abilities just to have food and shelter."

"Or protection," Maguire added.

***

"Did you ask your grandmother about tonight?" Anna asked as she and Angel made their way to the supply floor in the silo.

"Yeah. She said you need to stop by to let her know it's okay."

"I don't see a problem with that. Do you mind if I invite a couple of people?"

"Who?" Angel asked somewhat defensively.

Anna blew out a frustrated breath. *Two steps forward, dance back five.* "Jennings and Kim. I want to make sure someone has your back after I leave."

After a long moment, Angel nodded. "Lisa and Nelly? Sure. How about that woman from breakfast this morning?"

"Cy? No, I don't think she's anywhere near the slumber party type."

"Yeah, you're right. She probably makes s'mores with a flamethrower or something."

CHAPTER FIFTEEN

"Knowledge is power and since they can't know all things, they collect knowledgeable people," Madras said. The trio was sitting in the living room area. "Some survivors weren't a part of the original planning of Day Zero, but have been easily corrupted in its aftermath. And those who proved to be not-so-willing? Their families have been taken hostage so that the authorities can squeeze the brainpower and expertise out of any genius who remains reluctant."

Prescott shook her head. "Still, the land, the water, the air, all are contaminated. Will they just continue to send people to work in the affected areas, like canaries in a coal mine, until they stop dying?"

"I believe the radiation contamination was kept to a minimum in the U.S., and by 'minimum' I mean maybe a couple million people, so that they could rebuild or initiate plans to rebuild before the Powers-That-Be die. The water supplies are probably not as tainted as you might think. The amount of flushing out from water main breaks would keep any contamination to a lesser level."

"What kind of initial military force does the Triumvirate have?" Maguire asked.

"There are four engineer companies, two engineer battalions, and one engineer brigade at JBLM. They have the equipment, experience, training, and resources to keep everything running," Madras said. "They have four major infantry divisions, which include two infantry brigades. They have a huge MP/SP division, which includes a regiment of confinement soldiers. They have one Ranger battalion and two Special Forces groups – and that's just the ones we know about. They have field artillery, combat aviation, military intelligence, support brigades, four separate medical and hospital units. Remember JBLM was the military's largest mobilization center, prepared for anything and everything and always on alert. Whatever JBLM didn't have before the attack, they have now after Scholtz's Triumvirate took charge."

"So, they rounded up everybody who was on board with their plans and brought them here," Prescott surmised. "What happened to all those who were already stationed here who weren't on board?"

"Sent on TDY to all different places, so that everyone else could be put into place," Madras said.

"Temporary duty? Of course, so everything would appear legit." Maguire nodded. "Send them on 'training operations.' Remove and replace." She glanced at Madras. "How long had Day Zero been plotted?"

"Since long before Scholtz was placed into the presidency," Madras answered. "This has been in the works for years. They just needed the right person at the helm."

"How did Segundo get mixed up in all this?" Prescott asked. "Turned out he wasn't anything like them."

"Yes, but if you didn't know what you now know, you would have believed he was exactly like them," Maguire said. "I was one of the very few who experienced the honorable side of him."

"He was a good man," Madras said, a hint of wistfulness in her tone.

"So, Dr. Madras, what was Segundo's master plan for opposing them, and how on earth are we going to pull it off?" Prescott asked.

"Ms. Prescott, I have been reactivating unit members for the past thirty days, ever since I was able to stealthily implement the programs that will assist the Resistance in this mission. I have been tracking down, updating, and sending operatives to designated locations to start recruiting and training others to take out first the scouts, then the forces, as they start to make their move east to colonize."

"You know that I'm not as gung-ho as Maguire. I'm stubborn and I'm scrappy, but I know my limitations. I also understand the dynamics of what's going on here. I'd love to be as optimistic as the next person – despite everything – but can you tell me *how* we are supposed to defeat a fully equipped military?"

"What if we had hundreds of Maguires?" Madras asked Prescott. "What if the pre-trained soldiers were selected because they have Maguire's focus, grit, intuition, and perseverance? Maybe we won't defeat the hand-picked lackeys, but you can bet your ass we will weaken and demoralize them. At the very least, we will stun them, because they are so arrogant. They are not expecting any opposition, certainly not anything major," she amended. "They expect to be hailed as saviors and welcomed with open arms."

"How much time do we have? Training a small group is one thing..." Prescott spoke from experience.

"From now until full implementation of the Triumvirate's plans. Best guess, six to eight months. Containment is limited for the time being."

"Just in time for spring," Maguire predicted. "Planting season, warmer weather. People will be moving around. Easy pickings."

"Exactly, Sergeant. And timed right, survivors will have already done the hard work towards restoration. We should probably take a little break now. I'm waiting for a couple of colleagues to arrive who will explain a little more about the inner workings of everything that is going on."

***

Anna carried the provisions she would be taking with her into town back to her cabin, then led Angel off in another direction.

"Where are we going now?" Angel asked.

"I want to show you a couple of places to go whenever you don't feel safe, or if you know something's wrong, but you can't get back to your grandmother."

Angel followed Anna through the training grounds, past

indoor instruction areas and the Quonset huts used as barracks, to a path that took them deeper into a wooded area of the compound. Just when it looked as if the compound's property was about to come to a dead end by the back wall, Anna stopped. They were standing before a pile of dead brush and fallen trees that was covered with a light dusting of fresh snow.

"Whiskey Tango Foxtrot, Cy," Anna said in a clear, cool tone.

Suddenly two large branches were pushed aside, and Cy stood before them, smiling. "Hey, Anna, Little Noble. What's up?"

"Little Noble. I hate that," Angel muttered.

Anna ruffled Angel's hair. "I guess we'll have to come up with something that's all yours, huh?"

"Gee, that'd be nice," Angel said, the sarcasm plain in her voice.

"Nice job this morning, by the way," Cy said to the teenager. She turned her attention to Anna. "What can I do for you?"

"A few things. Can we come in and talk?" Anna asked.

Angel eyed the pile curiously. "There's an 'in'?"

Cy looked back toward the camouflaged entrance. "Pretty good, huh? Maguire taught us well." She turned and gestured to the entrance from which she had emerged, following the two visitors inside and replacing the branches in their designated locations.

***

Maya Surgick looked exhausted. Her usually wide, alert brown eyes were dull and squinty. When she'd glanced in the mirror that morning, she had remarked to herself that she didn't have bags under her eyes anymore; she had a full set of luggage. Her once smooth skin had lines and tiny wrinkles that hadn't been there the week before, having been added to the ones that hasn't been there the week before that. Her smile, formerly quick and radiant, was now reluctant and somber. Maya was a specialist on Rapturists, having dedicated her adult life to researching the cult. She had lost her brother Michael to the crusade years earlier, and everyone else in her family to the final devastation months ago.

She entered the meeting room at Madras' cabin carrying her third coffee of the day in her 20-ounce thermal cup. She nodded at each of the curious faces and then sat down at the head of the large, oval table.

Madras smiled at Maya, then stood. "Maya, this is Staff Sergeant Maguire, who I told you a bit about, and her colleague, Ms. Prescott. Ladies, this is Maya Surgick. She will introduce you to the mindset of a Rapturist, which will help you better understand the third leader of the Triumvirate, Reverend Josiah Franklin." She extended her hand toward the emotionally fatigued, black woman. "Maya, they're all yours." Madras resumed her seat.

Maya folded her hands together and took a deep breath. "Where to begin? Is there anyone here who has never heard of a Rapturist or doesn't know who Josiah Franklin is?"

"Assume we don't," Prescott said briskly. "Give us a quick tutorial."

"Fair enough. Josiah Franklin is a 70-year-old minister that got his start from his Prosperity Gospel father, Jedediah, who really built the foundation of the empire by preaching to the TV screen for big bucks. He created the first mega-church. He got rich off of people by using God as the ultimate guilt trip and convincing the weak-minded that they could buy their way into Heaven. Josiah apprenticed with his father and later inherited his immense wealth, but it wasn't enough for him. He wanted to create something more controlling, more...widespread, so he came up with Rapturism."

"Josiah Franklin is a piece of work," Maguire said.

"And then some. But his brand of guilt worked very effectively. What better way to get people to fall in line than to promise them a heavenly reward if they toe the fanatical line?" Maya said. "Straight white men who identify as Rapturists believe they are called by God to exercise supremacy over any non-religious society by assuming power over governmental, cultural, and theological institutions.

Rapturists are a horrible blend of Dominionists, Reconstructionists, and Armageddonists."

"So basically, they believe in their supremacy, even over other versions of Christianity. They do not respect any religion other than their own." Prescott sounded bewildered.

"Correct. They glorify radical, extreme *'Christian'* nationalism. They are in the same group as those who believe that the United States was founded for the purpose of being a Christian nation, despite the history and research that says otherwise. This gives them every reason to reject the cultural origins of our country's democracy. They firmly believe that the Ten Commandments and biblical principles should be the law of the land."

"How is their mania any different from the others?" Prescott inquired.

"The oldest male is the head of the family, and all fall into line behind him in terms of sovereignty. The patriarchy ladder is, say, great grandfather, next oldest brother, and so on, if he exists. If not, after the oldest male passes away, the rule goes to the oldest son, oldest brothers, then their sons, then grandsons. Always the oldest male."

"Where does the female come in the pecking order?" Maguire asked.

"She doesn't. Ever. If the oldest male in the extended family is a newborn, he has more power than the oldest woman, even if she's the great-grandmother. The pastor of the church heads the family until the oldest male becomes able to assume his role and responsibilities."

"If there are any of them left besides Franklin, they're certainly going to hate us," Prescott said. "Do they believe in multiple wives?"

"Actually, no. They believe all women are subservient to men, and all women must serve any male upon request in every way except sexually. That is a sacred bond between husbands and wives only." She sipped her coffee. "Like Reconstructionists, Rapturists are devoted to three areas of rule: church, family, and then secular, and only secular because they needed to stay aware of the enemy's motivations and actions."

"We are the enemy?" Prescott asked.

"Everybody who isn't a full Rapturist is the enemy."

"Sounds to me like all women with free will are their enemies," Prescott commented.

"Anybody with a free will that doesn't align with their covenants are the enemy. But yes, they especially reject women who don't *'know their place'*."

"If the women submit to the dominant male, who does the dominant male submit to?" Maguire asked.

"God, allegedly, but usually it's to whomever holds the ultimate power, which means the bankrolling. In this case, Josiah Franklin."

"Well, Franklin always thought he was God anyway, so I guess that makes sense," Maguire observed wryly.

"I never realized that Rapturists were such a powerful political movement," Prescott said.

"They had such momentum because it *wasn't* all political. They believed they were an ecclesiastically-guided movement boldly proclaiming a doctrine of total global conversion and dominance. They existed to enact God's laws."

"Isn't that known as 'theonomy'?" Madras asked.

"Theonomy is more Reconstructionism and Mosaic Law—the idea that the laws of Moses should be followed in a modern society. Rapturists go one step further."

"One step beyond, to believing that breaking any biblical law should result in an automatic death penalty?" Prescott asked.

"Yes. Rapturists believe that Old Testament biblical punishment should be meted out to those who break biblical law. But only Franklin could hand out the sentence. It was pretty barbaric when it happened. That's why you saw very few members who ever left or disobeyed the laws of the cult."

"Wait, they believe in Old Testament laws?" Maguire asked. "Like the Tanakh?"

"Pretty much. With the Christian adjustments, of course," Maya answered.

"Okay, that's confusing, because most of these people

are anti-Semitic assholes. Why would they align their religious doctrine with a faith they believe is inferior, written by people they hate so much?" Maguire asked.

"Franklin and the elders have brainwashed them all into believing that Christians wrote the Old Testament and the Jews stole it and took credit for it."

"I'm not religious at all," Prescott said, "but wouldn't they see the error of that dogma if they actually *read* the Old Testament?"

"It doesn't matter what they read, if any of them actually read," Maya said. "Franklin and the elders interpret scripture for them and tell them what to think."

"Then what's the difference between the various religious groups you mentioned?" Prescott asked. "Because they all sound pretty similar."

"Dominionists and Reconstructionists wanted to occupy all secular institutions and run everything from within, while the Rapturists, like the Armageddonists, seek to bring about the End Times by whatever means available. The Armageddonists didn't have a specific agenda, other than bringing on the destruction of the world, regardless of whether the catastrophe was political, financial, environmental, or religious. Rapturists needed it to be, or at least feel as if it was, Divine Intervention so they could go to their heavenly reward."

"How did Franklin get hooked up with Scholtz, the least biblical man on the planet?" Prescott asked.

"Power." Maya shrugged. "Franklin had the control and the money, but Scholtz had the power. Since they are both major scam artists, it was a natural fit."

CHAPTER SIXTEEN

There were three small bedrooms in the cabin, but Angel wanted to settle on the parlor floor. Being that the sleepover was her idea, she got what she wanted. Angel settled her sleeping bag in Anna's compact living room, opposite Lisa Jennings and kitty-corner from Nelly Kim. She had brought old-fashioned, stove-top popcorn with her to be cooked over the wood stove later in the evening.

Jennings had scrounged a box filled with packets of powdered hot chocolate mix from the MRE supply area, and she had brought enough for everyone to have at least two mugs each.

Kim brought a deck of cards.

Anna entered the room carrying a pitcher of mulled cider and a tray of homemade potato chips. She placed the items on a short stool next to her, where everyone else could also reach them.

Kim reached for a handful of chips. "I thought you might like to know, Jennings and I are next on the list to get our own cabin, so we'll be moving into yours in the next couple of days."

"Great. It's a good location." Anna smiled. "Close to the activity, but far enough away that you won't get a lot of the noise."

"Hey, Anna, can I go into town with you?" Angel took a gulp of her cider.

"To what? To live?" At Angel's nod, she said gently, "No, kiddo, I'm afraid not."

Angel shrugged. "It didn't hurt to ask."

Jennings grinned. "No, it never hurts to ask. But what's up? I thought you and Big Noble were getting along much better."

"We are, but...she's boring," Angel finished in a rush. "Anna's not."

"Don't worry, Little Noble, you can hang with us," Nelly said.

Seeing Angel's eyeroll, Anna cleared her throat. "We need to come up with a better nickname than Little Noble. She hates it." Anna patted Angel's arm. "Right?"

"Right," Angel responded. "Hey, maybe we could do that tonight—find me a new nickname."

"Before or after I teach you how to play Black Jack?" Kim asked.

"Why would I want to learn Black Jack?" Angel inquired.

"You want to play with the big girls?" Jennings asked. When Angel nodded, Jennings said, "Then you need to pay attention to Nelly."

"You want to learn how to *win* against the big girls, then you need to listen to Nelly." Kim began to shuffle the cards. "The game of Black Jack is similar to life. It's a game of chance, but there are strategic tools that can even your odds and, in some cases, make them better. You need to come to the game knowing the rules, prepared, calm, and level-headed. You must have patience and tenacity. You need to calculate theories of absolute and relative probability. You need to know when to risk and when to walk away a winner, and when to quit, even if that means temporarily losing." She looked at Angel. "Ready for your first lesson?"

"Yes, I am," Angel said around the handful of potato chips in her mouth.

Rapt at Kim's summary, Anna's hand shot up. "Me, too."

***

Late in the evening, when Maguire and Prescott returned to the meeting room after a quick supper, they found Madras talking with Maya and another woman. The newcomer was short of stature, wearing thick, black-rimmed glasses that seemed to suit her geeky appearance. Her hair was dark, braided and pinned up off the back of her neck. She reminded Maguire of Captain Jack Sparrow, without the facial hair.

"This is Remonna Becker," Madras said by way of introduction. "She is an Air Force veteran and held a highly classified, top secret government clearance. Like me, Remy pretended to go along with the plan for the new world order, but she openly defected to the Resistance when her wife was killed in the initial attack. According to the doctored reports, Remy died at the same time as her wife. That was a great loss to the Triumvirate, as she was one of their resident experts on nanotechnological warfare."

"So…they are okay with women not being subservient in areas where they can be useful to the cause," Prescott observed.

"Oh, no," Maya said. "They still expect all women to be subservient. If they have a valuable area of expertise, they must work under the eye of a male chain of command, who will take credit for any and all research or application women like Remy bring to them.

"Remy lives and works in what is officially listed as an abandoned warehouse on the other side of the lake. It was initially used as a storage area for the surplus of what they have at JBLM," Madras continued. "Remy, I turn the floor over to you."

Becker stepped forward, then adjusted her glasses before she spoke. "Thank you, Elaine." Her voice was husky, scratchy, as though she had smoked way too many cigarettes in her forty years on the planet. She turned to Maguire and extended her hand. "Sergeant Maguire, it is an honor to finally meet you. You are quite a legend."

Maguire accepted the woman's hand, shook it briefly and released it. Becker's fingers were dainty, but her grip was firm.

Prescott chuckled. "Legend, huh?"

"Yes, Ms. Prescott. My wife made contact with her at Panmunjom in what used to be North Korea. The sergeant was all she could talk about after their unit ran into a small mess and Sergeant Maguire got everyone out of it alive."

"What was her name?" Maguire asked softly.

"At the time, she was Senior Airman Andrea Shaye. She was a Tech Sergeant when she died. She—"

"She was a laser guide tech, and one ballsy woman." Maguire smiled at the memory. "Me and my MPs were coming back from a convoy escort when we got a radio call to back up some Air Force ground zoomies having issues," she said. "Those non-pilot personnel were mostly shot up because some feckin' idiot sent them out without enough fire power. We took care of most of the NK resistance, called in evac, and were ready to call it a day, but Senior Airman Shaye insisted on completing her mission. They were to laser paint a sensitive target ten more klicks out; she wouldn't take no for an answer. In fact, she called me 'an off the boat, fucking Mick' as I recall, and made some rather rude comments in reference to my parentage."

Becker made a sound that was somewhere between a laugh and a sob. "She wasn't always tactful."

"No shite," Maguire said blandly. "I split my team—half escorted the Air Force wounded, the other half came with me and her. At her mission point, we are taking a shite storm of fire and there she is, cool as can be, leaning over a fecking ledge with that damned laser pointer while my radio dog is calling in the air zoomies for their bombing run. She held that damn thing steady as I'm hanging on to her fecking belt. Small mess, my arse." Maguire had to chuckle. "Did she get her Silver Star?"

"She did. She was so proud of it." Becker did a double-take. "*You* put her in for that, didn't you?"

"She deserved to be proud. She more than earned it. And yes, I did. Your wife had a double serving of courage," Maguire said. "I *do* remember her, and I am so sorry for your loss."

Remy's smile was melancholy. "Thank you."

"Okay..." Madras sounded reluctant to end the reminiscence and yet slightly impatient at the same time. "As I've said, there's a lot of information to go over, so let either of us know if you get lost or have any questions. Time is of the essence, as everything needs to be strategized and in place before we can put our plan into action."

Remy nodded as she added, "The small warehouse I live in has several surplus, older model 3D printers, or as we call them, Additive Manufacturing."

"And what good does that do us, specifically?" Maya Surgick asked.

"It gives us access to making a great many things that we need, all good," Becker said with a smile. "Do you have any idea how many materials can now be printed with? They are too varied to list, but, just for example, the machines can print using stainless steel, bronze, gold, nickel steel, aluminum, and titanium. They can also print using ceramics, carbon fiber, and nanotubes—"

"What's a nanotube?" Maguire interrupted.

Becker glanced at her. "A tubular-shaped molecule composed of carbon atoms."

"That's about as clear as mud," Prescott observed.

"We can come back to that if necessary. The machines can print food; they can even print stem cells, for Christ's sake," Becker said.

"Stem cells? What? How long have we had that capability?" Maguire asked.

"At least five years. And they have the capacity to print in large quantities." Becker's fingers flew over the keyboard in front of her then pressed 'enter', and computer images projected onto the wall.

"That's great, but right now we have more immediate issues to deal with than finding cures for diseases. If we don't find a path to surviving the proposed strategy of the Triumvirate, cures won't be necessary," Surgick said. "So, again, what good is having access to 3D printers for *us*, specifically?"

"We can print unmanned aerial vehicles, complete with engines and electronics," Becker said succinctly.

The occupants in the room were silent a moment, absorbing that information, then Maguire's eyes widened. "Wait... Are you saying we can print drones? We can print fecking drones? With an explosive package? To drop on the heads of our targets?"

"Yes! We can print drones, we can print weapons, we can print ammunition, we can print nanotechnology." Becker's enthusiasm grew with each example she listed.

"Like nanoenergetics? Nanoexplosives?" Maguire was almost giddy at the possibilities.

Becker nodded. "Yes."

"If I understand it correctly, nanoexplosives generate over twice the power of regular weapons, which means smaller apparatuses have greater destructive power." Maguire started. "Meaning—"

"Meaning if we can produce these weapons, we can make them sneaky enough that they won't betray their arrival or give any warning before they accomplish whatever mission we program them for," Madras said.

"Exactly. In fact, it gets better," Becker added. "The nanocarbon tubes substantially reduce the weight usually needed to create a strong framework, which significantly increases the range of UAVs!"

"UAVs?" Maya asked.

"Unmanned Aerial Vehicles," Maguire translated. "Won't we still be limited by battery power, though?"

"First, we can apply nanomaterials to batteries to augment their reserve space, and that can almost quadruple the available power," Becker explained. "Second, we have come up with an inexpensive way to coat products with a super-thin, nonmetal element that exploits radar and light waves. These advancements in energy storage, components, and combustibles positively affect the variance, payload, and stealth of the UAVs. And," she nodded at Maguire, "using nanoexplosives will double the destructive power of the weapons."

"But without satellite access to track and control them, what good will they do us?" Maya asked.

"We do have satellite connectivity, which means we can use GPS for basic autonomous programs," Madras said.

"So, it would be like the unmanned K-MAX logistics helicopter used in Afghanistan. I remember Szabo talked about that once and said it rocked." Prescott looked at Becker for confirmation.

"Similar technology, yes, but this is much more advanced. Using the K-Max in an open area would be fine, but GPS has been inadequate and easily jammed for operations in narrow outdoor or indoor environments and dense urban areas. Fortunately, we have new inertial and visual navigation programs that overcome those limitations," Becker supplied.

"Could it get a drone to the target area and then direct the drone hit a specific target?" Maguire asked.

"Yes. With optical recognition, it can use multispectral imaging to identify a distinct object, such as an aircraft or ground fuel transports," Becker answered.

"This is amazing. Why am I just hearing about this?" Prescott griped. "I had a top-secret security clearance at Sansleau, and AI was one of my areas."

"The project was under Close Hold status," Madras replied. "Developers and researchers were put under a gag order to not talk about the testing, manufacturing, or use of these weapons."

"Why?" Maguire and Prescott chorused.

"Because these weapons are not vulnerable to interference or jamming, and they require no external input other than the identification of the selected targets. They also don't need human intervention. They can be pre-programmed prior to launch, and they can even travel to the area of the target but stay concealed until a specified time or until a specified target is recognized. That's not the kind of intel you want your enemies to have, nor the kind of information you want to give to anyone who isn't directly involved in the program." Becker waited for additional inquiries.

"So, basically, in the wrong hands, this kind of AI could teach itself to be autonomous and become like...what? Skynet in The Terminator movies?" Prescott asked in amazement.

"Something like that, yes," Madras confirmed.

"Wow." Maguire looked thoughtful for a moment. "Can these drones hunt mobile targets on their own?"

"So long as the general area is pre-programmed into the drone and an identifier can be recognized and locked into. GPS tracking made that part easier," Remy acknowledged.

"And all of this was going on right under our noses." Prescott sighed.

"Yep, and probably facilitated through deals made via the Dark Web by future members of the Triumvirate, using channels only available to certain qualified and secure members of the government," Maya added. "The average civilian would be horrified if they had any idea what they don't know."

"The use of these and similar weapons were deployed on Day Zero. That's why everyone was caught off guard. The gnat-sized intelligence drones were specifically surveillance and communication appliances that were so stealth, no one paid attention to them, especially when the larger and more terrifying WMDs were grabbing all the attention," Madras explained. "It gave the drone operators the data they needed to know when the most advantageous time was to send in the birds of prey drones. In terms of payload, range, and selectivity, these UAVs got into the areas the Powers-That-Be didn't want totally uninhabitable and took out large populations."

Becker took up the narrative. "3D printers made it possible to produce composite materials, energy densities in gel fuels, and nanoexplosives so that we were able to build longer range, more powerful, and stealthier drones. They deployed these drones in large numbers, which provided a particularly nasty challenge for existing ground forces and were another reason we were caught off guard."

"Well, that, and the fact that the attack came from within, so there could be no DEFCON warnings or even defense preparedness, like with NORAD," Maguire said. A second thought hit her. "Since the attack came from within, they could just mimic the warning system by cyber spoofing the program and making everything appear to be holding normally at DEFCON 5."

"Exactly. After years of scaring us about external evil forces, we became our own worst enemy," Maya commented.

"Okay, so you have control of this 3D-thingy warehouse," Prescott said. "That's all well and good, but how do we move what we make from there without getting caught?"

"Piece by piece," Becker answered matter-of-factly. "And it's not just the warehouse we have control of. The crappy news is that our enemy has a much larger warehouse with the monster 3D printers. These things build the birds of prey size UAVs. I'm guessing they probably have the room to print a fucking tank if they needed to."

Prescott blinked. "Well, that's reassuring."

Maguire smiled. "Blow the larger warehouse in place." She raised her hand for silence when they all tried to speak at once. "We've already established that Segundo was not a stupid man. He once told me that everything we would need to build and mobilize a counterattack would be in place. We blow the main warehouse and every bloody thing in it, making it look like a natural accident. Sabotage the 3D printers in the smaller warehouse so that when our fecking bad guys use them, those printed materials will fail in epic fashion. Then JBLM will no longer have easy 3D printing capability. The rest of what you want, and need, is at NORAD." She sat back with a satisfied grin. "Now I know what that genius meant when he said we'd have to give them nothing and have everything we'd need." She sighed aloud. "Segundo, you magnificent bastard."

Prescott blinked. "What?"

"Everything *we* need will already be at NORAD." Maguire repeated slowly. "We take away what large printing capability the enemy has, he can't fully or easily replace it. Once we have completed our mission of securing Cheyenne Mountain, we print as we need. When we begin our main attacks, the opposition will realize they are going to need additional weapon manufacturing, this warehouse will be important to them again and they will use sabotaged printers, which will produce less than optimal equipment."

"That makes a hell of a lot of tactical sense." Maya said quietly.

116

After a silent moment of consideration, Madras nodded, and then turned to Becker. "Tell them about the cube satellites."

"Wait, cube satellites? They aren't new," Prescott objected. "We used them at Sansleau."

"What are they?" Maya asked.

"Let me take a step back in order to answer that question," Prescott said. "Scientists wanted to study things such as the effect of space weather on radio transmissions or GPS, but the satellites that were necessary to do that were owned by major corporations or by governments. Major computer companies sold half-meter resolution imagery to anyone who could afford it. The development of cube satellites enabled non-government, scientific investigators to do research without having to pay the cost and licensing of using an established satellite. A cube sat is a miniature satellite made up of multiple cubic units. Cube sats are also what allowed us limited communication only days after Day Zero."

"The key, as you stated, is who could afford it. Yes, it was more cost-effective than using the full corporate-owned sats but it still wasn't cheap. And the rate of how many times a day the cube satellite would revisit a target was troubling, because the clarity of the image would be compromised with a lesser number of passes. Not only that, the host company could monitor what the consumer was looking at and automatically figure out what the consumer wanted to see. Then, unless the viewer was familiar with what they knew they should be seeing, the host company could be showing them anything," Becker said. "That would compromise the data the consumer was receiving, depending on the integrity of the company providing the information."

"We used cube sats to track all air, rail, port, and road activity in real time. The images certainly seemed authentic to me. Some of those areas I knew up close and personally, so, they clearly didn't send false coordinates to the contractors," Prescott said.

"True, probably not with certain government contractors, especially Sansleau," Becker said. "However, that was when cube satellites served as stabilizers on larger crafts. Just before the Triumvirate's initial world-wide attack, the U.S. government launched, and now use, an entire spaceport, which allows for more accurate and instantaneous information."

"Also," Madras added, "we can hack into any of their surveillance functions. That way, we can see exactly where they are looking and what they see."

"Since we can hack into their surveillance system, we should also be able to create a ghost program so that they are seeing only what we want them to see," Maguire said.

"We are presently working on that. Mr. Segundo recruited some of the best hackers in the business." Becker smiled. "Present company included."

"If our illegitimate government already has all these capabilities, how do you propose we get away with anything, much less an overthrow?" Maya asked. "We can't be naïve enough to think they don't have the people or programs to detect whatever hackers would attempt to do to their systems."

Madras grinned. "That's the beauty of it all. They are so arrogant that they truly believe they have eliminated everyone who could mount a military challenge to them. They believe that there were not many people left alive outside of the protected areas, much less anyone with the necessary skills and training. Anyone who did survive should have died quickly or been knocked back to the Stone Age as far as equipment and food were concerned, so they aren't worried – at least not yet – about any confrontational response that could make a dent in their new world order."

Prescott gaped. "They can't *actually* be that stupid!"

"Stupid? No. Clueless? Yes. Their hubris is their worst enemy." Madras sat back and stretched. "Let's call it a night. I think you must be at max absorption for now."

"For now?" Prescott repeated. "There's more?"

"Oh, much," Becker said.

Chapter Seventeen

The next morning, Maguire was up and about early. Not hearing any of the others, she stretched and did a cursory workout to loosen her muscles. Afterwards, she went to the kitchen area, and found that Remy Becker was also up, and had made coffee. She poured herself a mug and nodded her thanks. "What's on the agenda for today?"

Becker stirred milk into her cup and seemed to be contemplating Maguire's question. At last she said, "I believe Elaine is going to set up communications with some of the Resistance leaders. That will mean a stealth trek to the off-base warehouse where the 3D printers are kept. That building has been specifically jam reinforced by some of our audio crew so that no communications, or incoming or outgoing data from that location can be monitored by anyone at JBLM main. That's where she contacted Noble from, looking for you."

"How do you know it's secure?"

"Because, just like the Triumvirate had before the attack, we also have people working on the inside at JBLM who track all communications that are received, sent out, and intercepted. Most of the intercepted transmissions are from survivors with limited resources who are not a threat; they're just trying to find other survivors."

Maguire took a sip of her coffee. "I agree with Maya. I find it all so freaking bizarre that we were our own worst enemy."

"Yes and no. I think anyone who was paying attention – and I do include you in that category – could have connected the dots about what was festering barely beneath the surface of world politics. I believe that's why there was such a big fuss made about the dangers of the radical Islamic terrorist bogeymen, and the subsequent misdirection that everyone should keep their eyes peeled for menacing looking foreigners with turbans or hijabs."

"And the brown people south of our borders, and the black street gangs in Chicago," Maguire added.

"Correct. The average citizen was made so afraid of the 'other', that he never gave a thought to what was in his own front yard."

"Right," Maguire agreed. "And here we all thought Scholtz was a bloviating idiot."

"He is, and he isn't. He's also nefariously cunning, and he surrounded himself with ambitious and knowledgeable people. In the political shell game, he didn't need to be the hand that was moving the misdirecting objects, he needed to be the pea under the nutshell."

"More like the nut under the nutshell." Maguire leaned against the kitchen counter. "Do we know what their sea resources are like? Nuclear subs, naval warships, aircraft carriers? Do we know what's still out there and functional?"

Becker smiled. "Once again, we can thank Mr. Segundo for his foresight. Last year, he was involved with the launching of a subsurface glider that gains and stores energy from the sea thermocline. It is estimated that the subsurface glider can function for five years without refueling."

"Wait," Maguire tilted her head in thought, "I actually heard something about that. It's a small, unmanned, underwater research probe, right?"

"Right. It can patrol for weeks following foundational directions and commands, then surface intermittently to report and receive new orders. It has demonstrated that it is capable of travelling a global range while producing very little in the way of repetitive patterns or characteristics."

Maguire chewed that over for a moment. "So, it appears as a blip on sonar, but it's unidentifiable?"

"If it even registers on sonar. It's quite a stealth little vehicle." Admiration was clear in Becker's voice.

"Who did Segundo oversee this project with? I'm military. I know that something like that can't be accomplished totally under the radar."

"It was designated as an experimental program and came to fruition with the assistance of the Navy," Becker said. "There are three of them patrolling the oceans in different parts of the world, and we have access to the stats from all three. We know what they know."

Moving beyond the obvious intel-gathering functionality of the gliders, Maguire asked, "Can they be armed?"

"Yes, but that would be difficult. They are monitored by the Triumvirate, so any data upload or download, or any longer than normal stationary coordinates would alert the Powers-That-Be."

Like a dog with a bone, Maguire persisted. "But in the meantime, until we can figure out how to make them work to our advantage, we can still see what Naval forces are operational and who they belong to, yes?"

Becker smiled. "Yes. As well as what their capabilities are."

"Sweet." Maguire downed the last of her coffee.

***

Prescott uncrossed her arms. "Okay, I'm impressed that we have – or will have – access to hundreds of—"

"Thousands, actually," Becker corrected.

"*Thousands* of UAVs," Prescott acknowledged. "But do we, will we, have the logistics or enough trained individuals to successfully deploy and direct them?"

"We have enough people to train others, if need be," Becker said.

Maguire looked skeptical. "Will we have the time to train?"

"Most of it would be on the job, so to speak," Becker admitted. "Most everybody today knows how to use controls or a keyboard to work a toy drone or a video game. It's basically the same concept. We can reprogram the UAVs to be IEDs that actually hunt specific forces in the fields."

"Not to mention seeking out vehicles, helicopters, and sea vessels, as well as their ammunition and fuel dumps,"

Madras added. "We can use the 3D printers to combine the IEDs with the UAVs, and use the Triumvirate's programming against them. We can start by programming wave attacks by the hundreds to hunt ground targets, and then go from there as the battle progression dictates."

"If we can do that to them, what's stopping them from doing that to us?" Prescott asked.

"Nothing." Madras said. "Except their belief in their infallibility."

"Do we have the capability to enable these devices to self-deploy if the human operative should become incapacitated?" Maguire asked.

"I don't see why not," Becker said. "I think we should be careful with that technology, though. Like you said, if we can get them to do that, so can the Triumvirate. We don't want to give them any ideas."

"Then we would just have to plan a surprise attack and swarm them first, disabling their fleet," Maguire said. "Do we have intel on the locations and outposts of Triumvirate forces?"

Madras nodded. "We have hacked into several solar-powered balloons that are still providing internet connectivity. They can rise to an altitude of about seventy-thousand feet above the Earth and provide us with surveillance, which will assist us with gathering any topographical intel we need."

"Why can't we defeat them cyberly?" Prescott asked. "I mean, if we can cripple their power supplies and their digital capabilities, wouldn't that be half the battle?"

"It could help, but I doubt it would actually slow them down. They have a clearly defined mission, and they have considered every component necessary to accomplishing that mission," Becker said. "The main thing we have on our side is the element of surprise."

"We're doing a lot of talking, but not a lot of doing. I say we get this show on the road," Maguire said. "The longer we take to pull this Resistance together, the more time they have to organize and put their stakes down and gain territory and momentum."

"Quite right," Madras agreed. "We need to hit them before they can implement any of the plans they have for extending their domination. That will be the key."

***

Angel was reluctant to leave Anna's cabin, but she packed her sleeping bag and left with Jennings and Kim early the next morning. She didn't have a new nickname yet, but she was open to hearing options. Anything was better than "Little Noble".

The previous evening had been enlightening for her, and she had gained a new admiration for Kim, blackjack, and especially Jennings, who showed her a few unarmed self-defense moves. She was determined, now more than ever, to make herself a productive member of Sanctuary's defense team. She also had come to an awareness that maybe her gram's ideas weren't so lame after all. For the first time in her young life, she felt like she belonged.

***

The darkened warehouse smelled less musty than Maguire had expected it would. When Becker switched on a solar powered light, the illumination revealed a cache of large, assembled 3D printers, a healthy reserve of unassembled 3D printers, and an arsenal of reinforced and labeled steel tubs containing various plastic filament, powders, alumide, resin, nylon, stainless steel, gold and silver, titanium, ceramic, gypsum, and anything else needed to complete whatever project proved necessary.

Becker led the group into another section of the warehouse that held an entire wall of computer monitors. The screens displayed camera surveillance of what Maguire guessed was not only different areas of Joint Base Lewis McChord, but data that appeared to be running statistics of daily activities and troop movement within that facility and Yakima Training Center. Remy stopped between the two men overseeing and operating the display terminals.

"This is D'Andre Rancifer," she indicated a young black man with dreadlocks, "and this is Frank Inglis," she gestured to a middle aged, balding white man with a mustache that resembled a bristle brush. Neither man acknowledged the introduction, as they were intently keeping an eye on the monitors. "We don't know everything the Triumvirate is doing, but we've got a lot of really good intel. We can also scan their communications traffic, which is invaluable."

Prescott moved closer to the console. "This is really impressive. And they have no idea this building exists?"

"Oh, they know it exists," Madras said. "They just believe it is an unmanned surplus and storage area, and therefore useless." She walked over to a row of dark computer terminals, selected one, activated it, and began to type in commands.

"Are two people all you have monitoring everything that is going on?" Prescott asked, incredulous.

"No, there are others," Becker assured her. "This is the time for mandatory prayer at both Yakima and JBLM, so activity is currently at a minimum."

"There is mandatory prayer now?" Prescott squawked.

It was Maya who answered. "Sure. The military is theocratic now. There are mandatory prayers twice a day."

"So, two different times, every day, everyone is required to stop what they are doing and attend worship," Maguire repeated thoughtfully. "Doesn't that leave them vulnerable? If they are all occupied with praying, who's minding the store?"

"There are soldiers who are granted special dispensation to miss prayers, so as to not leave vital areas unattended. They usually rotate those soldiers out every couple of weeks, though, so that they can participate in invocation. Remember, these zombies are indoctrinated to feel 'less than' if they miss prayers. Also, by rotating them, no one gets stale and complacent in their duties," Maya added.

"Maguire," Madras called out, "someone wants to talk to you." She motioned Maguire to come over to the computer bank.

When Maguire came into view of the monitor, she grinned at seeing Joseph Red Horse on the screen. The visual was a bit snowy because of interference with the camera connection, but the audio was clear. As she sat down at the terminal, Red Horse was smiling back at her.

"Let me guess, you're on the team." Maguire's voice was laced with hope.

"Long before I had any idea. Same as you, I guess. What was your code word that triggered you?"

"Trodaí. Irish Gaelic for Warrior. You?"

"Histã'u. It's Athabaskan. It loosely translates into the phrase 'it is woven'."

"It is woven," Maguire repeated. "As in, 'it's been told'?"

Red Horse shook his head. "Eh...more like, 'it is in the fabric of history'."

"Looks like he tailored a code word for each of us." Maguire felt Prescott at her side and introduced her and Red Horse to one another.

"So, what do you think of this mess?" Prescott asked him.

"Well...thanks to Segundo, it is not the enormous cup of suckage it could have been. We know our enemy, and although they seem like single-minded, domination-focused ignoramuses, they are not to be underestimated." Red Horse scowled. "Despite our collective disdain for them and their objectives, the people in charge are all white men from entitled educational and socioeconomic backgrounds, with sophisticated degrees from distinguished colleges and universities, some with extensive military training."

"But Scholz isn't one of them. He's a puppet of the extreme neocon movement," Prescott said. "He can barely string words together to form a sentence."

"He must be still useful to them, or they would not even keep him as a figurehead. The question is, in what manner? In the meantime, we have to be concerned with a specific mindset of people who didn't successfully get to this place by being uninformed and unworldly in their way of thinking. Their method of brainwashing was effective, and now knowing exactly what it takes to control the fringe, they can use it even more productively to their advantage." Red Horse continued, "Whatever they said and did made sense to their diehard base, because they were convinced that the Scholtz Administration wouldn't lie to them."

"But their government did lie to them," Prescott objected.

"Yes, just not in the way they led them to believe," Red Horse said. "Everything sinister was blamed on the imaginary Deep State, which played into the fringe's fears and bigotry, and all the while the Triumvirate was setting in place exactly what they pointed fingers at others in the 'secret government' for."

"I get it," Maguire chimed in. "They passed themselves off as intellectuals with so-called strong foreign policy, trying to save the world. What they hid from everyone except those of us who sought or knew the truth was that they were all about power. Morality and ethics never entered into the equation."

"This is why we have to take into consideration the way in which they successfully manipulated the media and how completely their base swallowed their lies," Red Horse said. "*We* didn't see them as the saviors of the world because we knew better, but their fear mongering and outright lies played right into the dreads of those they were attempting to dominate'"

"Namely, the entire world," Prescott said.

"God, we are a gullible species," Maguire groaned. "People underestimated their powerful devotion to military and paramilitary measures, cloak-and-dagger operations, coordinated provocations, subtle intimidation, economic influence, and the mass manipulation of the press." She scrubbed her hands over her face in frustration, then thought to ask, "How's Las Cruces?"

"A ghost town. Those murdering bands basically all killed each other."

"So, your mission... I won't ask you what it is exactly, but will we meet up anytime soon?"

"I have to, um, *procure* some areas you and Jessica already traveled through so that we can secure facilities with which to maintain a stronghold. Over the last couple of months, small governmental militias have settled on the properties to, I assume, guard them until the military begins its movement eastward."

"Think they'll be a problem?" Maguire asked.

Red Horse gave her a confident smile. "I am not worried. Just a bunch of religious redneck bullies who are too pompous for their own good. Kind of reminds me of Yellow Hair Custer." He grinned. "As for meeting up, it will happen exactly when it is supposed to, but hopefully, sooner rather than later."

Chapter Eighteen

Angel slithered under the bushes, ignoring the minor scratches she was acquiring. The white sheet she'd wrapped around herself blended in with the recently fallen snow. Once she was in place, she settled down to wait. Jennings had told her that being a commando took a lot of patience, because there was a lot of time involved in watching and doing nothing. After five minutes, Angel had to agree with that assessment. She let out a sigh.

As the minutes piled up, Angel found herself not exactly daydreaming, but thinking about the future and what she wanted to do when she grew up. *If I grow up.* She mentally shook the thought from her head. She knew that she didn't want to lead Sanctuary. She'd seen what that had done to her grandmother. And she was well aware that she had not been much help. She cast her eyes down in shame, sucked in a breath, and promised herself that she would do better. *Is nearly freezing in the bushes a part of doing better? Yes,* she decided. *Yes, it is.*

Angel did not like or trust Carrie and some of her lieutenants. Not just because of how they treated her, but because of the way they talked about her grandmother when her gram wasn't around and, most recently, their threats to Anna. And, since the militia and the commandos had been created, Carrie had been mouthing off more often than usual to the guards who didn't like the two new groups. Fortunately, even more of them had been talking about leaving the guard to volunteer for the new units. It made her smile that even though her grandmother ran the place, people pretty much forgot that *she* was around and could hear them. It was like she was a piece of the furniture.

Moving slowly, Angel checked her wristwatch. Two hours had passed, and she was beginning to think she might be wrong, that she might be wasting her time watching the back of Carrie's cabin. Also, her curfew was in an hour. She really didn't want to miss curfew and give her grandmother a reason to not trust her. She was about to leave her stakeout when the back door opened and out stepped Carrie, Patnode, and Dettmer. Angel wondered why Malcom wasn't with the group. Usually she was joined to Carrie's hip.

Angel was bothered by the way the women were furtively looking around. Usually those three strutted boldly anywhere they went, hardly ever even taking notice of anyone other than themselves. Right now, they were skulking. She watched them until they disappeared from sight. She wanted to run after them, but instead she forced herself to stay still, just in case they turned around and came back. When she had counted to fifty, she slid out of the hiding space and followed their tracks as best she could. She lost the trail at the gravel path that led to the showers, and she debated whether she should follow, or go for help.

It took her less than five seconds to make her decision. She turned and ran as fast as she could to where she knew she would find some of the commandos.

***

Anna picked up the last items she was taking with her and loaded them into the wagon. It didn't amount to much, but it would be enough to sustain her for the time being.

Jennings had brought her the radio, solar charger, and battery Noble had promised and was now seated on the driver's bench, anxiously reminding Anna that it was almost dusk. Anna knew Jennings could take care of herself, but being outside the compound after dark, alone, was not advisable for even those most able to defend themselves. Although there had been no attack, or any evidence of one being planned, it would be tempting Fate to travel outside Sanctuary when there was no illumination other than that provided by the moon. Rogue bands of Scholtz supporters and surviving lone wolves were alive and well in some outlying areas. So far, they had left Sanctuary alone, but it would have been foolish to think the residents were safe outside the walls after twilight.

Anna took one final look at the cabin she had shared with Maguire and Baumer, and a flood of memories washed through her and tears filled her eyes. She took a deep breath, wiped away the tears, and hopped up on the bench with Lisa.

"Let's go," Anna said, and Jennings made a clicking noise that started the horse clopping toward the gate. Anna glanced down at the M16A1 rifle that occupied the space between them. She knew it was locked and loaded, and she found comfort in its presence. She smiled as she recognized the major changes she'd undergone from the naïve person she had been before the devastation that had changed life as she had known it.

They left the compound without incident, and as the gate closed behind them, Anna smiled, looking forward to being in town with Doc. She found Doc extremely attractive. She would admit to having a small crush on him, but that was because she felt safe with him. He was a genuinely nice and caring man, but she didn't believe she had any serious romantic feelings for him.

"Boy, you're deep in thought. Anything you'd like to share with the class?" Jennings said.

Anna blushed, and then wondered why. "No, not really. I guess I'm wondering how different it will be not living in Sanctuary."

"It should be fine. There appear to be no problems in town, and Doc seems to be a decent guy. Plus, he'll be able to focus on teaching you what you need to know, since Noreen and the others just didn't have the time."

"Or the patience," Anna added, knowing that she sometimes wasn't an easy student.

"And, you have the radio," Jennings continued, "so all you have to do is call if you need anything."

As they rode in companionable silence, Anna enjoyed the wintery landscape they were slowly passing through. She pulled her coat more tightly around her and was bent over to re-tuck her pant leg into her boot when she heard a sickening crunch and then an "oof" from Jennings. The well-trained horses halted as soon as the reins hit the ground. Anna sat up quickly and watched with horror as Jennings fell from the wagon seat. She lay still on the snow-covered ground, blood seeping from a head wound.

Anna scanned the area and spotted three figures dressed in the uniform of Noble's militia, including black balaclavas that covered every part of their heads except their eyes. The armed trio quickly approached the wagon, two with their handguns trained on her and the other covering Jennings' still form. Anna grabbed for the rifle beside her, and one of the voices shouted, "Don't!" Anna's hand stopped before she touched the weapon.

"Keep your hands where I can see them and get down off the wagon!" another voice ordered.

She stood slowly and climbed down from the wagon. The two voices she had heard were female. As the trio approached, Anna observed their mannerisms and determined them all to be women. "What do you want?" she asked, struggling to keep her voice from trembling.

The third person said to the one who was now hovering over Jennings, "Leave her. Get that gun."

Anna recognized that voice. It was Carrie's. She also had determined that the person following Carrie's order was Dettmer. She hadn't yet figured out who the third person was. "You're not off house arrest. How did you get out of the compound, Carrie?" Anger began to replace Anna's fear. "Dettmer help you escape?"

"Not your concern, sweetheart." Dettmer picked up the M16 off the bench where Jennings had been sitting, and then jumped down to the ground. She bent down and felt Jennings' neck for a pulse. "She'll live," she announced.

"Well, you were pretty accurate with that rock throw, so maybe she won't ever be right in the head again," Carrie said smugly.

The utter disregard made Anna shudder. "Look, I've left the compound. What is it you want?"

Carrie strolled up to her and stopped entirely too close for Anna's liking. Anna refused to take a step back, though, and hoped her expression was as defiant as she intended it to be.

"You owe me." Carrie's voice was low, her tone, ominous.

"No, I don't. You created your own problem. If Noble didn't think your behavior was unacceptable, she never would have disciplined you."

"Well, Noble isn't here, is she? Neither are Prescott or that maniac Maguire. Now you answer to me." Carrie bumped her chest hard against Anna's, knocking her off-balance and to the ground.

When Anna started to scramble to her feet, Carrie stepped forward and unleashed a vicious kick to Anna's midsection that knocked the breath out of her and crippled her with pain.

"Stay down," Carrie commanded.

Anna was terrified. Jennings was incapacitated, and Carrie's team had all of the weapons and the advantage. Halfway between Sanctuary and town, she was at Carrie's mercy. Something inside her morphed into rage and she forced herself to her feet, but she didn't stand still. She fired off a right hook that caught Carrie on the side of her face, and Anna felt a flash of satisfaction.

Carrie's fist connecting with her diaphragm didn't take Anna by surprise as much as that it happened more quickly than she was thought it would. Doubling over, Anna gasped for breath as she was yanked back to a standing position. Laughter loud in her ears, another fist found her left kidney and pain blossomed. Then the beating began in earnest, continuing until Anna was lying on the ground and struggling to maintain consciousness.

"I'm having fun, how about you?" Carrie sneered.

Anna struggled to her knees and straightened her back, smiling up at her attacker past bloody teeth. Two sets of hands lifted her to her feet.

"What the fuck are you smiling at?" Carrie shouted.

When she didn't get an answer, she crooked an elbow and drove it against Anna's head.

***

Dettmer released Anna, who fell almost bonelessly until the back of her head hit the ground. Dettmer looked from Anna to Carrie. Half a second later, Dettmer was staring at the arrow that had slammed into her chest.

Carrie grabbed the front of Patnode's shirt, pulling her forward while at the same time stepping around behind her to use her as a shield. An arrow caught Patnode in the throat, and she fell to the ground. Unshielded, Carrie ran as hard as she could, slid under the wagon and rolled out on the other side, then disappeared into the darkness.

Her compound bow loaded with another arrow, Cyclops rushed out from the tree line and slid on her knees to a stop next to Anna. A wave of relief surged through her at seeing the young woman's chest rising and falling. She glanced over at the two women she had killed, feeling only disgust for them.

"Bixby coming in," came a shout from the tree line. A moment later, Charlie squad leader Nancy Bixby emerged through the trees. She quickly checked each masked woman. "Dead. I'm going to check on Jennings. Ortega and Nix are just behind me."

Cy nodded, all the while keeping an eye on the opposite tree line, just in case Carrie decided to show some courage. She doubted that would happen.

***

Anna awoke in a haze, paralyzing pain washing through her and making her violently nauseous. Throwing up only made the agony worse. When she was done evacuating bile from her empty and bruised stomach, she closed her eyes to stop the sensation of spinning. When she opened them again, they were finally able to focus. She watched as Noreen dipped a cloth in a bucket of water, wrung it out, and then gently laid it against her throbbing temple. Anna tried to thank her, but her throat burned and her voice was a raspy whisper.

"What...happened?" She closed her eyes at the sharp streak of fiery pain that raced along her hairline.

"We're not exactly sure," Noreen told her calmly. "Maybe you can help clear that up for us when you feel up to it."

Anna took a deep breath against another wave of nausea. Images slowly began to form in her mind's eye of being kicked bloody as she lay in the snow. Her next recollection was of Jennings also bleeding in the snow, and her eyes shot open. "Lisa! Where is she?" Anna choked out.

Noreen looked up as another person entered the room. "Go get Rachel," Noreen instructed.

Anna reached over and weakly clasped Noreen's wrist. "What happened to Lisa?"

"Jennings is in the next room. She's faring better than you are. She has a nasty concussion but is otherwise fine."

Anna breathed a sigh of relief at knowing her friend was safe.

***

Rachel Noble sat in a chair by Anna's bed, her normally stoic features flickering between worry, frustration, and barely contained anger. "How are you feeling, Anna?"

"Like I got caught on the ground during a stampede. How long have I been out?"

"You've been in and out of consciousness for nearly a week," Noble told her.

Anna's eyes grew wide with shock, which made her head hurt. She squinted at Noble. "What?"

"Yeah. We were getting a little nervous. Are you up to talking?"

Anna gauged her pain, dizziness, and nausea. They were all still there, but not nearly as overwhelming as they had been earlier. "I'll talk as long as I'm able, though I'm only recalling flashes of what happened."

"What do you remember?" Noble prodded gently.

"Um…" Anna closed her eyes as though that would help bring her memory back. "I was being kicked and beaten."

"Do you remember by whom? Was it one person, or were there more?"

"I think there were two." Anna concentrated. "At least two."

"Did you recognize them?"

"I…" Anna hesitated while her mind conjured up images of balaclavas. Then eyes. Then voices. "Yes." The mental picture of the moments just before the attack became clearer. "There were three… Carrie, Patnode, and Dettmer. It was Dettmer who hit Lisa with the rock."

"Are you positive?"

"Yes." Anna was certain of her memory. "But it was Carrie who beat me."

Noble sighed and stood. "Thank you, Anna."

"Wait. I have some questions. How was Carrie allowed out of the compound?"

"She wasn't. She sneaked out with the help of Patnode and Dettmer."

"How did we get back here?"

"Quarterman and her crew got there just in time. They brought you and Jennings back to Sanctuary."

"Quarterm— Oh, Cyclops," Anna figured out. "What were they doing out there?"

"Quarterman reported that Angel saw Carrie and the others leave, and she ran and told the commandos."

"Angel did that?" Anna tried to smile, but it hurt. "I'll have to thank her."

"She'll like that."

"Someone let Doc know, right?"

"Doctor Porras has been out to check on you once a day," Noble said with a smile.

"And what about Carrie and her crew?"

"Dettmer and Patnode were killed. Unfortunately, Carrie is in the wind."

With deliberate concentration, Anna took in Noble's

demeanor. She was almost vibrating with simmering rage. Anna wondered whether Noble was more upset by the betrayal of Carrie and her pack, or by knowing that she would have to tell Maguire about their attack when she returned from Washington.

CHapter Nineteen

It was the kind of night that defeated even the best wet weather gear. Slashing rain found every opening in their covering and soaked them down to their socks as Prescott and Maguire slogged up to the front gate of Sanctuary and gave their mission password to the Sergeant at the gate. A second armed guard unlocked the gate and let them enter.

"I'll give Noble a shout." The duty officer reached for the com box. "By the time you get up there, she'll be waiting."

Prescott took two steps forward, then halted and turned around. "Isn't Carrie normally the one who's on this shift?"

Shifting uncomfortably, the guards exchanged glances but neither responded.

"She asked you a question. Answer it," Maguire growled.

The sergeant cleared her throat nervously. "There have been some changes in personnel. Carrie is no longer Captain of the Guard."

Maguire nodded. "Thank you." As they continued squelching through the mud toward Noble's office, she grumbled, "Join the Army, my Da said. Should have listened to my mother."

"Yeah, well it could be worse."

Maguire raised an eyebrow. "How, exactly, do you figure that?"

"Well, you could have been a dentist. Imagine all those germs, sharp teeth, screaming people, magazines two years out of date, and Fox News on the TV in the reception room."

Maguire missed a step and nearly fell. "Do you stay up at night, thinking of things like that?"

"No. They just come to me," Prescott answered without

hesitation.

They tramped in silence for the last quarter mile. On Noble's porch, they dropped their rucksacks, shucked out of their rain gear, then knocked on the door.

The night Charge of Quarters let them in and pointed them to the coffee urn while she went to get Noble.

The heat of the coffee cups warmed their hands, and the extra sugar in the coffee was an attempt to stave off their exhaustion. They were halfway through a cupful when Noble came out of her room and opened the door to her office.

"Shawna, no disturbances unless the place is burning down or we're being attacked," she ordered. She followed Prescott and Maguire into the office, then closed the door. "The two of you look as bad as the weather. Anything you need before we talk?"

They both shook their heads as Maguire reached into her pocket and pulled out a waterproofed packet.

"To put it bluntly, we are in a world of suckage." She took one flash drive from the packet and placed it on Noble's desk. "From Madras. The other copy is for us to take with us, so that we can make a copy for any ally we might encounter."

Prescott leaned back in her seat and closed her eyes. "Rachel, if you had told me a year ago what's on there was true, I would have laughed in your face and then punched you for suggesting it."

Noble eyed the flash drive warily. "That bad?"

"Worse," Prescott croaked. "You wouldn't believe the level of..." She shook her head in despair.

"Collusion," Maguire finished. "Do you recall back in the bad old days of the troubles in Northern Ireland—the collusion between the Brit army, *Intelligence* services, the RUC and the Prod *paramilitary* groups?" Her voice was hard, caustic.

Noble nodded. "In our intel section, we called it 'the quiet murder sanction'."

"Well, that was a picnic on a beautiful day compared to what you'll read here," Maguire stated plainly.

Noble sucked in a quiet breath. "Suggestions?"

"You read it. I need a shower and some chow." Prescott leaned forward slowly, stiffly. "I shouldn't have sat down."

"Take an hour, then come back. I'll skim as fast as I can, and you can walk me through the rest of it. We'll make decisions from there." Noble looked at them with an unfathomable expression, then cleared her throat. "You should know that Anna will be leaving Sanctuary and moving into Doc's house. Carrie is no longer Captain of the Guard. We will also discuss that when you return."

Maguire bolted to her feet. "Is this something I'm going to have to kill Carrie over?"

"You'll have to get in line," Noble answered honestly. "Go get cleaned up. I'll see you in an hour." She picked up the flash drive and plugged it into her computer. "Why are you both still standing here?"

***

Prescott took her usual seat across from Noble's desk, a small plastic plate filled with bacon-flavored seitan and biscuits balanced in her hand. She chewed on a slice of the wheat meal meat substitute as Maguire entered carrying a fresh mug of coffee. Both were dressed in clean uniforms.

"Don't get comfortable," Noble ordered as she walked in and dropped into her chair. "I radioed Mugnier and Barton and sent them copies of the data via email, double encrypted. They've been reading since, and are expecting us. We leave in fifteen." She looked at them intently. "Are you absolutely sure that what is on this drive is accurate?"

"As one hundred percent certain as we can be," Prescott answered honestly. "As much as I hate to say it, Rachel, it fits."

"How can you be so sure?"

"Madras knows her own family most likely died in the attack. She sacrificed them to deportation so that she could get inside the circle. That much is public record. When I read the story in the papers, I thought she was a right cunt for turning them in," Maguire admitted.

Noble closed her eyes and pursed her lips. "Don't use

that word."

"Which one?"

"Maguire, I am not in the mood. Guess which word I absolutely hate. It's right up there with the n word," Noble snapped.

"Right," Maguire muttered. "The world is ending around us, we're on the verge of being killed or becoming slaves, and you're upset about a word."

Noble said nothing for several moments. When she spoke again, she returned to the principal focus. "We have no choice but to move forward with this information." She turned her chair to the window and gazed out. "I cannot believe that all of us, the entire world, are victims of treason at the highest level."

"I can't believe only a select few figured it out," Prescott said quietly.

Maguire cleared her throat, and the other two turned to look at her. "They've been working for years to lay the foundations and implement their plans. Segundo told me, us, that those who saw something coming were silenced. Some had 'accidents', some 'committed suicide', and some were just called conspiracy wingnuts."

"And still no word from Mr. Segundo?" Noble asked quietly.

"No. Madras doesn't know why, and she can't ask too many questions, despite her position." Prescott bit into a biscuit.

Noble nodded. "Second item—Carrie."

"What happened?" Prescott asked around a mouthful of food.

"Before I tell you, I am giving you both an order and I fully expect you to obey it, upon penalty of expulsion. Even now, in these current circumstances. Neither of you, nor any person you might designate as your agent, will go after Carrie."

"First of all, let me remind you, again, that I do not take orders from you." Maguire's words were clipped. "So, my response to what you have to say will depend primarily on what it is that Carrie has done to Anna."

"Maguire, Anna is safe," Noble assured, "so Carrie isn't a priority, especially now. I am asking you to please place all other issues on the back burner and concentrate on this mission. Can you do that?" Noble knew she was playing on Maguire's focus being mission-oriented, and was grateful when Maguire didn't disappoint her. It took a long moment, but both women nodded.

"Carrie did inflict injuries on Anna," Noble stated flatly. When Maguire instantly bristled, Noble held up her hand before either of Anna's friends could speak. "Doctor Porras diagnosed a severe concussion, but he expects a full recovery. Carrie is on the run. Don't think I haven't dispatched anyone to track her, because I have. Maguire, your commando-trained soldier, Nix, has been tasked with tracking Carrie. Finding Carrie will probably take time, and what we have going on right now requires our complete focus, but never doubt that Carrie will be found, and she will face Sanctuary justice."

Prescott smacked her plate down on the table. "Details?"

"We don't have enough time." Noble held her hand up again, forestalling an onslaught of questions. "You will get all the details after we get back from the generals' compound. That might be a while, but I promise that I will not withhold any information from you. I want you to know that no one is very happy with Carrie right now. In the two and a half weeks that you have been gone, we have seen a little bit of why your Jessica decided to keep Anna with you to the end of your journey," Noble finished quietly.

The tinny sound of an ancient Jeep horn forestalled any objections, and Noble snapped, "Let's move, ladies." She grabbed a small backpack and slung it over her shoulder, then held the door open and gestured for Prescott and Maguire to precede her out of the office.

Prescott turned back to Maguire and flashed a grin. "Now you know what I still see in her." Then she was out the door.

Maguire blinked and shook her head, not making eye contact with Noble. "I didn't need to know that." She took a last sip of her lukewarm coffee, set the cup on the desk, and quickly followed the others out to the Jeep.

***

"We read it." General Mugnier's voice was rough and soft at the same time. "Rachel, are you certain that this intel is legitimate?"

"As sure as we can be. Mr. Segundo's actions regarding Sergeant Maguire, the training program and, in retrospect, some of the other things he was appointed by the President to 'oversee'... It all fits, Al. God!" She considered her next words carefully, wanting to make a strong case, but not wishing to insult these military men who could be their first allies. "The aligning with the extreme Religious Right was bad enough. The deals made with the Russians and the blatant lack of response to Russian military activities before the final destruction of peoples and property... God help me for saying it, but it all supports the allegations that the President committed high treason and is complicit in a conspiracy to commit mass murder."

For several moments, the only sound in the room was the ticking of the clock and the rasp of measured breathing.

"I never did like or trust that draft-dodging, supercilious son-of-a-bitch," General Mugnier snarled, and then took a deliberate, calming breath. "Brendan, you spent the most time at the Pentagon. Options?"

"It depends on what we have to work with." General Barton looked at Maguire. "Staff Sergeant, sit rep."

"In addition to the instructors, there were twenty-eight of us in Segundo's program, Sir. I'm not sure you can count the instructors, though. We moved around from base to base, so it might be just us twenty-eight who had any idea about the true purpose of our training. So, we have the twenty-eight, and any of their people who will follow them. I know we can count on our El Paso allies, Ramon and Victoria Lejos. Red Horse and his faction from near Las Cruces are already on the move. Exactly where they're going, I am not privy to just yet.

From what I have been given to understand, all the Resistance leaders trained in Segundo's program are at least fourth generation Native American. We have to be careful not to feck them over."

Mugnier's eyes flashed, and not in a good way.

"Let's be honest, Sirs. All due respect, you white guys have fecked it up for centuries. Your ranks will be respected, but you will not be in charge this time around." Mugnier and Barton looked shocked, but Maguire stood resolutely behind her statement.

"As always, Sergeant, you are bucketful of insubordinate sunshine," Mugnier finally ground out. His eyes shifted back to Noble. "Do you have a plan, Rachel?"

"We gather who we need, both peaceful and armed, where we need them, and centralize the Resistance. Communications, intelligence, and even black ops, as much as I hate to say it. If…when the traitors come out of their holes, we need to be adamant about not turning the other cheek. There's always one idiot who wants to *talk* to the other side, to be the peaceful diplomat. We are beyond that. If Elaine is correct, we will be outnumbered and outgunned, so we must strike first."

"For the most part, I agree with your assessment. I suggest two central locations for Resistance headquarters. If they silence one, we use the other," Mugnier plotted. "Split coms, tactical operations, and supplies in order to serve both locations at the same time. Define a rally point if we have to fall back."

"With satellite locations for distraction, harry, and harass," Barton added. "We'll need intel and counter intel. And Psy Ops on double time. Al, your recon boys are going to be busy. Maguire, so will your operators. If your commandos are trained Ranger-style, then necessary quick strikes will come fast and heavy."

"As to that, gentlemen," Noble said, "on the way here, we discussed the three primary objectives as outlined by Dr. Madras. One is taking control of NORAD without giving ourselves away. Ramon and Victoria Lejos will be vital for satellite image analysis. I know Ramon. If anyone has cyber backdoors into the system, it's him. As for finding the three additional hackers as Madras has requested, I'm not sure what she had them working on, but if she wants them found, then it's important. I suggest we combine personnel to form a strike force to accomplish those three missions."

Mugnier and Barton froze like rabbits caught in a motion-activated spotlight, both blinking repeatedly. Maguire and Prescott reacted with similar surprise.

"Rachel, did you just suggest—" Barton began.

Noble stiffened and fixed them with a direct gaze. "Yes, I did. Gentlemen, the needs of today are more important than things that happened yesterday. In an effort to ensure that we reduce the potential for any unfortunate incidents, I recommend that Maguire ask for volunteers from the ranks. I fully expect that there will be some women who will refuse to share space with men, and there will also be some men who still believe women are inferior. By asking for volunteers, we would be culling most of those people from the get-go," she finished.

"Thank you for your trust, Rachel." Mugnier's tone was soft, thoughtful.

"And if they don't behave themselves, I'll just gut them." Maguire's smile indicated she actually meant what she had said.

Noble groaned.

"God, you're an asshole," Prescott muttered.

General Barton grinned at Maguire. "Outstanding. Go Army."

Maguire arched an eyebrow. "I was talking about all of 'em. Including mine."

Chapter Twenty

When Maguire and Prescott entered Anna's room in the infirmary, it was already quite crowded with Angel, Jennings, and two thirds of Charlie squad. The conversation faded into silence as Prescott closed the door. It was almost painful to see the bruises on their young friend's face, and the huge lump and dark stitches on Jennings head.

"Leave you alone for ten minutes," Maguire drawled in a casual tone as she gave Anna a careful hug.

Anna winced as she attempted a smile. "Can't take me anywhere," she quipped.

"She is still slightly nauseous, and she said her head is pounding," Jennings supplied.

"Do you have any Irish in you, Anna?" Maguire asked.

Anna blinked. "Not that I know of."

"Then quit leading with your head. That's reserved for Micks." She turned to face everyone else. "Charlie squad, thank you. I'll never be able to repay this gift you've given me." She dropped to one knee beside Angel and looked her squarely in the eyes. "Angel Noble, I am forever in your debt."

Angel nodded once, then cleared her throat. "I want to learn to be one of your commandos," she requested, her voice cracking. "I know I'm not old enough to be an...an active member of the squad, but I still want to learn."

Jennings cleared her throat. "I'm willing to teach her."

Bixby snapped to attention. "I'm on board."

Ortega was the next to stand. "I'm in."

Cy stayed seated, so relaxed that she almost looked to be asleep. "I'll teach her to shoot. It took guts to do what she did."

Anna slowly raised her hand. "Guys, maybe someone should figure out who's going to run this idea past Noble."

Angels face immediately fell. "She'll never let me." Defeat was clear in her tone.

"You'll have to ask her," Prescott said quietly. "You want to put your butt on the line to insure the future of Sanctuary, the best way to convince her you can make a contribution is for you to do the asking."

"She'll never let me," Angel repeated quietly, leaning back against the window sill.

"Are you sure, or are you making an assumption?" Prescott prodded. "The first part of leadership is asking hard questions, even when you might not get an easy answer. You also might have to have a backup plan in case you get shut down."

Angel looked confused. "What do you mean by that?"

Prescott tilted her head in thought for a moment. "You want to train to be a commando, even though you know full well that everyone believes that at some point you will be the future leader of Sanctuary—"

Angel jumped to her feet. "But I don't want—"

"Don't interrupt me, please." Prescott didn't snap, but her tone was granite. "As I was saying, when you ask your gram, you should do it as the possible future leader of Sanctuary, not as Angel Noble, granddaughter. That means that you will have to convince her that this absolutely isn't hero worship of some dirt dogs. And, you can't go back on your word and quit when you decide the training sucks. The Army doesn't work that way."

"Hooah," Bixby said quietly. When all heads turned to her, she shrugged and sat down.

"I've got to get to a shooting time I set up." Cy slid her dark glasses back onto her face. "Either way, kiddo, I'll teach you to shoot. I'll even face Noble to let her know, but Pres is right. You have to ask her." She stood up and braced to attention.

"Hit it," Maguire ordered.

"Almost every single time, Top." Cy grinned as she

grabbed her soft cap and exited the room, closing the door behind her.

Maguire shook her head. "If she wasn't so damn good at hitting shite…"

Bixby laughed and stood. "I'm taking Charlie out for three days. We'll scout around and try to contact Nix. No promises."

"Roger that. Good hunting." Maguire watched as the rest of Charlie squad quietly departed, then she turned back to Anna and Jennings. "Where'd you go wrong?"

"It's my fault." Jennings cleared her throat. "I assumed that Carrie was secured, even after Anna gave me the lowdown on some of her shit antics."

"I didn't want to make a fuss, and I definitely didn't want to give Carrie the idea that I was scared of her," Anna added quietly.

"Were you scared of her?" Prescott's voice was uncharacteristically gentle.

After a long moment, Anna nodded. "Yes. I was."

"Scared is okay. We all understand scared. Jennings, you ever screw the pooch like that again, I'll bury you myself." Prescott's eyes were hard. "Alive. We clear?"

"Crystal clear, Staff Sergeant," Jennings responded crisply.

***

Maguire led her commandos into the Quonset hut used by Mugnier's Recon company for briefings. They dropped their rucks on the floor near the front door and quickly settled into the seats sitting vacant for them. Without being instructed, her commandos sat at attention, as did the Recon Marines already in the room. Maguire caught movement at the back door of the hut. A split second after noting the silver bar about to walk in, she snapped to and in her parade voice barked, "Atten- TION!" The entire group rose as one.

The female Marine First Lieutenant didn't blink as the group snapped to attention. She pulled her cover off and tossed it on the desk as she halted in front of the assembly.

"Take your seats," she ordered and waited for both units to sit. "For those of you who do not know me, I am First Lieutenant Kimbrough. The scary man who will be joining us is Gunnery Sergeant Cortez. We will be your evaluators.

"Staff Sergeant Maguire, Recon is lending you five snipers, so pick five spotters. I understand you have three snipers, so Recon will provide you three spotters. The rest of you will pair off, one Recon to one commando." She took a moment to look at each person seated. "You all knew what you were getting into when you volunteered. Staff Sergeant Maguire will be in overall command. Recon element, if you have a problem with that, you can turn in your boonie hat and shoulder tab. That is a direct quote from General Mugnier. Non-Marine element, you will refer to me as Lieutenant Kimbrough and to Gunnery Sergeant Cortez as Gunnery Sergeant Cortez. Recon has earned the right to shorten our titles, you have not."

When a few commando eyes snapped to her, Maguire nodded, then addressed the group. "Non-commando elements will refer to me as Staff Sergeant Maguire. I don't care which element you belong to, I will deal fairly with any 'issues' across the board. If the issue stems from personality, we can switch out partners. If that doesn't work, I *will* kick your arse out of this detail.

"Evaluators will be handing out the course guidelines. We have roughly six weeks to figure out how to work as a team—three weeks in garrison followed by three weeks in the field. I will see that you have at least two off days, so you can get your shit together."

Maguire allowed them a few moments of silence to process any thoughts they might have floating around in their heads. As she waited, a large structure of a Hispanic man entered the hut and pulled off his cover. She would have sworn she heard several of her commandos gulp.

According him the respect he had earned, Maguire snapped to attention. "Good Morning, Gunnery Sergeant Cortez."

Half a second later, the entire group replicated her

greeting. The medal that hung at his throat suspended by a blue ribbon entitled him to that honor. Generals would snap to attention when this soldier entered a room.

"Commando element, this is Gunnery Sergeant Cortez," Maguire intoned. "And yes, that *is* the Medal of Honor hanging around his neck. If you haven't figured it out, when he comes to you wearing the medal, you will snap to attention. He has earned that. If you don't, I will eat your heart for breakfast. When Gunnery Sergeant Cortez is not wearing that medal, you *will* listen to him. He is a bigger bad ass than I'd *ever* hope to be."

"Scare the shit out of them, why don't you," Cortez grumbled in a harsh tone. "I will be conducting evaluations, and I will be enhancing your hand-to-hand combat skills. I don't have a lot of time for bullshit."

That said, he began handing out pages of mission guidelines to the assembled group. Maguire and Lieutenant Kimbrough grinned, gravitating closer to one other as the some of the commandos eyed the Gunnery Sergeant in awe.

"I never get tired of seeing that expression," Kimbrough whispered. "Most of our Marines are used to him, but we still have some rookies who look at him like that."

"Did you not see my face? Saint Brigid deliver me, I never thought I'd be in the same room as a Medal of Honor recipient." She let out a slow breath. "He'll make my commandos better, I know it."

Kimbrough tried to stifle a snicker. "Who are you kidding? DSC and a female with a Commando tab? Please."

"I was having an extremely bad week when that happened, and I wasn't a Fionaglach at the time. Others bled so that eejits could try and pin that medal on me."

"And yet, Staff Sergeant, they *did* try to pin that one on you. You earned it, with help. Some of us know that. As we in the Marines say, "Suck it up, cupcake.""

Maguire grinned. "As we Irish say, 'Feck that.'"

Kimbrough's laugh was low, melodic. "You and Cortez are cut from the same cloth. Just so you know, he said you'll make Recon better as well." She watched one commando roll her eyes at her seatmate. *Interesting.* "Did you really skirt the

Recon boys three times?"

Maguire grinned slowly. "It was actually four, but I think General Mugnier would have had me shot if I had said more than three."

"General Mugnier cut his teeth in Recon, from baby L.T. in Desert Storm to 2013, when he finally had to take his first star. He hated leaving them for the circus in DC. He trained this force personally, and I'm not kidding when I say they are damn good," Kimbrough offered.

"Why do you think I had to move four times? They got within three hundred feet of us. If the wind had been blowing in their direction, they *would* have found us," she admitted. "Don't tell them that, though. Don't want them getting cocky. Mine won't get cocky, except maybe Cyclops."

Kimbrough looked at Maguire. "Cyclops?"

There was no humor in Maguire's voice when she explained, "The woman can't quit rolling her eyeballs."

"Ahh, gotcha. Saw her." Kimbrough sounded totally familiar with the type. "We have a few of those in the infantry. General Barton eats *those* for lunch. He like pancakes for breakfast." She grinned. "God, I love my job."

Maguire *had* to laugh at that. The woman sounded downright giddy, and she could understand the sentiment. Kimbrough probably did not get the opportunity to train and evaluate very often. "Welcome to my world," she offered, then sobered. "Who do I have to keep an eye on, or worry about?"

"Smythe. Give him to your overall best soldier. And let her know that she *can* bust his chops if she needs to. He's good but he's cocky, and he *is* an asshole. That being said, when you snap him back and rattle his brainpan, he gets it. It just takes getting his undivided attention. Sims is a close second. We cut him some slack because of his unfortunate background, but he's one hell of a spotter. You can't rattle that boy. I'd take him even over Smythe, depending on the circumstances."

"Unfortunate background?" Maguire repeated.

"Poor guy." Kimbrough's voice was quiet. "Started off

as an Army puke."

Maguire blinked. "Poor indeed. He had the best, and now he's stuck with the likes of you."

Kimbrough took no offense. "Oh, this is going to be the most fun I've had in forever. But all fun aside, give Sims to your best sniper. You'll thank me later."

Maguire snapped to attention. "Thank you, Ma'am. Permission to carry on?"

"Carry on, Army." Kimbrough snapped to attention. "All reports will be completed by the following morning. We can catch up after chow to review the day's activities."

"Roger that." Maguire turned to the mixed group, sucked in a deep breath, and barked, "Snipers against the wall to my left; everyone else, wall to my right. Now, children."

In moments, everyone was where she needed them to be. "Quarterman, raise your hand." Cy immediately did as instructed. "Recon Sims, that is your new best buddy." She consulted her notes. "Recon Fielder, raise your hand." He did. "Belton, you spot for him. He is your new best buddy." She continued through the roster until snipers and spotters had been matched.

"Smythe, raise your hand." It took a moment before anyone moved. When he finally did, Maguire eyeballed him. "You have a hearing problem, Smythe, or are you just slow?"

He barely hid a smirk. "I'm used to Marines, *Sergeant*."

Maguire nodded in mock sympathy. "Well, that explains the disrespect and the inability to follow orders." She walked over to his side, grabbed his left ear and twisted hard as she dragged him out of his line. "I am not as soft as your Marines, Smythe. When I call your name with instructions, you will fecking obey. Do I have your attention now?" she growled.

"Yes, Staff Sergeant Maguire." He almost managed to sound as if he wasn't in pain.

She released his ear. "Jennings, that shite is yours."

Jennings closed her eyes for a moment, but moved quickly to his side. "Hooah, Staff Sergeant Maguire."

Maguire could barely hear Gunnery Sergeant Cortez' laugh and his faint "Asshole."

CHAPTER TWENTY-ONE

Sims watched through the scope as a hole appeared in the target. "Low left. You breathing right?"

"I don't think I am," Cy replied. "It's a new rifle for me. I think I'm trying too hard," she admitted. "Or maybe my grip is wrong. Definitely not a relaxed grip."

Sims spat some dip off to his right. "Fair assessment," he said softly. "You got a girlfriend?"

Cy looked at him from the corner of her right eye. "What?"

"Me, I have a wife. Having her makes me more relaxed, no matter what I'm doing. Look down your scope." He waited until she complied. "Now, we just have to find out what relaxes you. You didn't answer my question before."

"No, not anymore," she admitted, looking down her scope at the target.

"Wanna dip?" he asked.

Cy laughed. "No."

"Wanna tell me why you're not breathing right? Why your grip is off?" he asked. "If we don't figure it out, I'm gonna miss dinner and my wife is gonna kick my ass."

"We wouldn't want that," Cy teased. "I've never fired a Dragonov before. I have no idea where Maguire or Noble got one. It's beautiful."

Sims suddenly peered at her. "Do you suck at this?"

"What? No!"

"You only give the best rifle to the best sniper. So, do you suck, or are you good enough for this gorgeous gun?" he prodded.

Cy started to retort, then thought about it. "I don't suck," she finally managed.

"Good. Start proving it." He peered through his spotter's scope. "Target, five hundred yards; wind right to left, swirling ten miles per hour. Ready?"

Cy took a breath and looked through her scope. "Ready."

"Fire at will."

***

Bixby dragged the unconscious form back to base and dropped it in front of Gunnery Sergeant Cortez. The unfortunate Marine Corporal had had the bad idea that Bixby was an easy target for intimidation. "One more of your jarheads tries to take advantage of one of my commandos, and next time I will reach into his chest and rip his lungs out. Are we clear, Gunnery Sergeant Cortez?"

"They have to learn sometime," he agreed. "By the way, how did you get that banged up eye?"

Bixby fumed. "He got in a clean shot."

"Keep your right hand up," Cortez advised.

Bixby snapped to attention and then turned on her heel. As she walked past Maguire, she allowed herself a small smile and a wink of her good eye. "I think it's going well," she said softly.

***

Maguire crawled into her bunk with a slow, painful breath. "Jesus, God," she groaned. It hurt to even blink. The last time she had hurt that bad, there were North Koreans involved.

A knock sounded on the frame of her tent. She didn't have the energy to answer with words, so she just groaned. In seconds, the front flap of her tent was swept aside, and Anna entered with a cup in hand.

"I heard you were training with Godzilla today." Anna almost managed to stifle the giggle. I thought you might need this." She held out the cup.

"Traitor. And that's Gunnery Sergeant Godzilla to you," Maguire managed, then took the cup. "This is going to taste like arse, isn't it"?

This time Anna didn't try to hide her amusement. "Oh, yeah."

Maguire gulped the tonic down in two large swallows and fought off the urge to puke. "Feck. You could try, at least to look sorry for that," she gasped.

"Not even pretending." Anna laughed loudly. "Payback for pushing us so hard on our original trip to Sanctuary." She leaned down and pulled the blankets over Maguire's lean frame. "Doc and I have called a day off for you and Recon. All of you need it."

Maguire shook her head. "We don't have time—"

"Take the time, you dumb Mick. You should be proud. I think a couple of Marines cried in relief when they heard about the temporary suspension of training."

Maguire felt whatever it was in the medicine starting to turn her muscles to Jello. Half stoned, she grinned. "Real tears or crocodile?"

"Gunnery Sergeant Godzilla grinned when he told me about it, and he spoke in an entire sentence."

"Real tears, then. All right. One day off," Maguire slurred, then blinked. "What the hell did you put..." A moment later, she was out.

***

"Trainor, get your ass over here."

Maguire's voice stopped the hand-to-hand exercise. Her commando dropped her head, knowing she was caught and, with no choice, ran up to Maguire.

"You will pack your gear and you will road march your fucking arse back to Sanctuary. I told you to control your punches. Your failure to obey has put me one Marine down, your own partner. Get the feck out of my sight." She glared at her commando. "Right after you apologize to Gunnery Sergeant Cortez and Recon Private Davis." She knew the order would eat at Trainor.

Maguire watched as the crestfallen woman apologized,

then left the practice area. Maguire faced the detail. "I told you," she barked, "that I would be fair. Anyone who disregards orders is gone. Private Davis, I will assign you a new partner, and you will bring her up to speed."

***

Maguire dropped her gear next to her desk and sat down. She wondered why Jennings was still standing to the side, looking like a child who had bad news to share. "Yes?"

Jennings cleared her throat, took a deep breath, cleared her throat again. "Uh…" She closed her eyes.

"I don't usually kill the messenger who drew the short straw," Maguire said dryly.

Jennings blew out a breath in frustration. "I know this isn't mission critical, but some of the others, they were wondering— Who are we?" she blurted out at last.

Maguire blinked. "Group amnesia?"

Jennings shook her head. "Those guys, they're Recon. Their uniforms have a tab saying so. They have those stupid looking, floppy boonie hats." She locked eyes with Maguire. "Who are we?"

The light bulb went on. "Ah. To tell you the truth, I have no idea. Since you are Noble's forces, I thought she would come up with something."

"She hasn't. It kind of sucks. We're supposed to be the ones going out there and making first contact, putting our asses on the line, and Noble hasn't done anything to acknowledge us. Some unit members are pissed off."

"Then they need to quit," Maguire snapped bluntly. "Crying over a lack of acknowledgement. Jaysus. Please take them back a message from me. I will do what I can, but in the meantime, get over it or get the feck out of the unit."

Jennings nodded but didn't move. She cleared her throat again. "They said, um, that if it can happen, they, um," she swallowed, then rushed out, "they'd like a beret."

Maguire blinked like an allergic squirrel. "Get the feck out of here."

Wisely, Jennings made fast tracks out of Maguire's

presence.

***

Noble sat back in her desk chair and just stared. "They want what?"

"Unit name, logo, recognition. And a beret. I mustn't forget the beret," Maguire muttered. "Stupid useless-ass covers."

"Then why do you wear one?" Noble's sarcasm was not at all disguised.

"Because I earned it. But it's still stupid and useless."

"Well, your black one is kind of plain, but the other one is different," Noble pointed out.

"Right. So, did you plan for berets and new unit patches and beret badges?"

"Not at all," Noble said dryly. "I don't know how I didn't make that my number one priority."

Maguire snickered. "Fecking Recon. Jealousy sucks. Best I can do for now is to call an all forces formation and have you conduct a pass in review. Say a few words. 'Your bravery in the coming days...' Blah, blah, that sort of thing."

"When did adults turn into children?" Noble's question was a mixture of annoyance and frustration.

"Well the *other kids* have the cool toys," Maguire deadpanned.

"I'll do a full Sanctuary formation, no pass in review. Somehow I don't think we have time for dog-and-pony shows." She rubbed her eyes. "Berets. I don't even know where we could get the damn things. We have a few women who have sewing and embroidery skills." She shook her head as she looked at Maguire. "And I have no idea whatsoever about what to call this force."

"Don't look at me." Maguire shrugged. "Everything I can think of has already been done."

There was a knock on the office door. "Come," Noble called out, glad for the interruption.

Prescott entered and closed the door behind her. "Can

someone please shoot me?"

Maguire obligingly started to draw her pistol, but received a warning glare from Noble. "What?" Maguire asked with feigned innocence.

"Now what, Pres?" Noble ground out as she leaned back in her seat.

"I hate logistics," she griped as she took the seat next to Maguire's. "How'd your day go, honey?"

Maguire blinked and threw her pen at Prescott. "Feck you."

Noble tilted her head back and looked up. "God, please tell me what sin I committed that I am being punished like this? It must have been a big one, but I don't remember it."

"Sorry." Prescott actually sounded sincere. "Here's the issue. We have to be in at least three different locations at the same time, and I don't see cloning in our future. Let's call Red Horse's area one mission, with two objectives in relatively the same location. NORAD, two missions split. Hunting down three hackers, one mission over a hell of a lot of unknown ground."

Noble nodded, then closed her eyes, thinking, remembering, plotting. She was doing what had made her career—seeing the small pieces and plugging them into the larger picture. Suddenly she opened her eyes and stared at Maguire.

"Contact Red Horse on his frequency and see if he can secure Ramon Lejos and his daughter in El Paso and get us a sit rep on Las Cruces."

"I talked to him my last day with Madras, remember? That whole area has changed, and his crew is already on it."

"Call him again," Noble persisted. "I want to be as up-to-date as possible on everybody's progress. I will try to contact Elaine to get more detailed intel. She knows these three hackers and where they might be hiding."

***

"I suggest we meet in Dulce, New Mexico, if you think you can make it. Over," Red Horse said into the radio mic, responding to Maguire's update.

"Dulce? Isn't that where they allegedly have that underground human-alien joint base?" Maguire asked. "I thought that was bullshit. Over."

"Not in the way you think," Red Horse said. "There are secrets there, but it's bullshit that it involves aliens. No alien lifeform would waste their time with a planet as hostile as ours. I haven't been there, but my intel says that it is a military operation experiment and the 'aliens' are actually earthlings from the future. Over."

"What?" Maguire thought about that. "Hmm, if it is true, does that mean we survive? Over."

Red Horse's laugh reverberated through the speaker. "Thank you. I haven't laughed in a week. Are all Comanche as easily deceived as you? Over."

Maguire ears burned with heat. "I officially hate you." She glanced up at the ceiling as she blew out a breath. "Okay, why Dulce? Over."

"Is this radio secure?" Red Horse's voice was now totally serious. "Over."

"Yes. Over."

"Some of your bad guys might have come out to play a little earlier than planned. They annoyed the Jicarilla Apache, on *their* rez. I'm pretty sure it didn't go so well for them. I'm running a courier up there as soon as we finish here. I'll ask the others about it, but I'm pretty sure those Z packs you and Jess shared will garner you volunteers. Over."

"Thank you, Captain. Over."

"I told you, I'm out of the Army. Currahee. Out."

As the connection ended, Maguire smiled smugly. "Out of the Army, my arse."

Chapter Twenty-Two

On his way to pick up supplies, Doctor Porras' thoughts turned to Anna, and the effect she was having on his life. Now that she had settled in with him, he had to admit his little house felt more like a home. And they seemed to be quite compatible as housemates.

He had an easy affection for Anna. He read no hidden possibilities into those feelings, because he held a similar affection for Prescott and even Maguire, as thorny as she could be at times. Although Anna had changed tremendously from the person she had been when they first picked her up, she maintained a sweetness that just couldn't seem to be knocked out of her no matter what she went through. He was thrilled, though, that thanks to the guidance of them all, mostly Jess and Maguire, Anna no longer took crap off anyone, especially Prescott, who had given her plenty. They were all family in this strange new world, and he was grateful.

Anna had also assumed the task of inventorying the contents of his make-shift stockroom. He hated that particular chore, and Anna was more than willing to take it on. They had most of the essential medical supplies, but the inventory count kept him up to date about what additional necessities he should obtain.

Doc approached the co-op with a small shopping list. As a town citizen with a necessary occupation, he could draw supplies without having to bring actual items to barter. At some time or another, he would be paying for his supplies by bartering his medical skills. He held the door open for a woman whose two young children had a case of the sniffles. He'd been to their house in the last week. When the woman had exited, he stepped inside.

"Hi, Doctor," Mr. Cameron called out from behind the counter. Two other patrons echoed the welcome.

"Morning, everyone," he replied as he picked up a hand basket. "I hope everyone is well."

No new medical ailments were registered, so he slowly walked the aisles, taking his time, picking out only what he truly needed. Since he often had an added bounty of supplies that Anna, and sometimes Maguire, brought him, he didn't want to deprive others of what they might need. His eyes swept over the candy bars, then back to his basket. A small taste of past normalcy called to him, and he could not resist. He carefully placed two Hershey bars in his basket. He'd share one with Anna and save the other for Angel when she visited.

"How's that young lady settling in, Doc?" Mrs. Blythe asked, her eyes twinkling. She was a widow, who, along with her daughter and grandson, owned and operated the town bakery. It was a small business, made even more modest by the events of Day Zero. She supplied all the baked goods for Mr. Cameron's store, for Sanctuary when requested, and also special orders for other folks. "I hear she's from the compound. We had no idea you were looking for a bride."

Doc felt his cheeks flush. He wanted to correct the misconception and say that Anna was more like his little sister, but if everyone thought he was 'taken', they might stop trying to fix him up with every eligible woman in town. Not that there were that many to begin with. On the other hand, he didn't want to put Anna in the awkward position of either playing along with such a charade or remaining uncomfortably silent about their friendship.

"We met before we found our way to the compound," Doc said vaguely.

"What took her so long?" Mrs. Blythe asked, her tone incredulous.

Doc grinned and shrugged, then tactfully excused himself. When he had collected the items on his list, he wound his way around a couple of shoppers to the counter, where he set the basket down.

"I swear, Doctor, you have got to be one of the most polite men I've ever met." Mr. Cameron chuckled. "You want to give lessons to my son?"

Doc smiled. "It's my mom's fault, and my fiancée's. They trained me well before the world went to hell."

Mr. Cameron's lips pressed together tightly, his typical reaction when folks talked about the dead or the past. "They did a damned good job, Doctor."

"You know you can call me Kyle or Doc," Porras offered with a smile.

"You're a doctor, you earned the title. I will not fail to respect that." The answer was almost gruff. Mr. Cameron emptied Doc's basket, then scribbled a list of the items and amounts on a receipt page. His eyes darted left and right, then back down to the page again. "You still go out to Noble's on occasion?" Mr. Cameron's voice was almost a whisper.

Odd. He knows that already. Doc's brow furrowed, but he nodded slightly. His volume matching Mr. Cameron's, he said, "Only when I'm invited. Perhaps now that Anna's staying with me, I might go when she goes."

Mr. Cameron slid a thin piece of paper on top of the receipt and folded all of it over together. "Well, Doctor, your total comes to three house visits for official purposes, and one visit that requires you to bring your stew," he said at his normal voice volume as he bagged the supplies and handed Doc the receipt. "Next Tuesday?"

Briefly wondering why the shopkeeper had folded one piece of paper inside the other, he nodded. "Next Tuesday. Invite your son, I'll try to infuse some polite." Doc tried to keep his chuckle from sounding forced.

Mr. Cameron displayed a tight-lipped smile instead of his usually toothy grin. Doc took his bag, exited the front door and held it open for another customer, then turned right down the street.

***

While putting away the items he had just brought home,

Doc reached into the second bag of supplies and pulled out the receipt. When he was finished storing the goods, he would give the receipt to Anna to put with his inventory. He placed the invoice on the counter and reached back into the sack, removing a package of cotton balls and what looked like another receipt.

Glancing at the second piece of paper, Doc saw that it was actually a note. He began to read, and his throat suddenly went dry.

"Anna," he rasped. "Please come here! I need you to take a look at something."

***

Porras stopped in front of the guardhouse and politely asked for a runner from Noble's office. He felt self-conscious under the eyes of the guard. Some of them still blamed "the Maguires" for Carrie's downfall. He took a page from Maguire's book, adopting a nonchalant stance while whistling Amy's favorite song. His fiancée had had a love for Evanescence, and had hummed or whistled each song ad nauseum. But now, it helped him stay calm despite the note that had been delivered to him by the shopkeeper. And now he had to relay its vitally important contents to Noble.

***

Noble read the note, let it fall to the top of her desk, and sat back in her chair. It tilted precariously. "You're sure of what this says?"

Porras shrugged. "You've known Mr. Cameron longer than I have. Is he a liar?"

Rachel shook her head. "I don't always like him, and we don't always agree. Actually, most of the time we disagree. But no, he's not a liar." She exhaled a long breath. "Damn it." She looked up at Porras. "Tell me, Doctor, is there anything you aren't willing to do?"

He was confused. "Ma'am?"

"You save lives, you stare down pink bunny slippers, and now you bring me secret agent messages." Noble's tone was flat.

Porras was not sure whether she was joking. "I thought you should know."

Noble cracked a smile. "And you have no idea how important this is. What do you know about Boyle City?"

He shrugged. "Nothing. I've never been there."

"Doctor, you and Mr. Cameron may have just saved your new town, and Sanctuary." She leaned forward. "I'd invite you to stay for coffee—"

"If that note means what I think it does," Porras interrupted, "I'll soon be busy, and so will you. I'm going to go get my office set up for whatever might be coming down the pipe."

"Thank you, Kyle," Noble said, as sincere as she had ever been in her life.

He stopped dead in his tracks, turned and smiled. "You called me Kyle. Do you know how long it's been since anyone called me Kyle?"

***

"Jesus Christ on a crutch," Prescott wailed in frustration. Noble had just informed her and Maguire of the warning Doctor Porras had brought. "This is definitely a distraction we do not need right now."

"I agree," Noble said, "but we can't ignore it."

"Understood. But what if reacting to this threat tips our hand to JBLM?" Prescott said.

"I don't believe it will." Maguire looked up from the detailed note Noble had handed to her. "This looks more like a ragtag bunch of neo-Nazis trying to establish some dominance and territorial control rather than something as organized as the Triumvirate. Besides, if this was actually the beginning of the expected move eastward, Madras or someone would have advised us."

"That's true," Prescott concurred. "So, I guess this means a full dress rehearsal for the actual show, huh?"

Noble looked at Maguire. "Do you think the special forces are ready?"

"They'd better be."

"I guess this will let us identify our strengths and weaknesses," Prescott said, accepting the note from Maguire and reading it again. "It will also evaluate how well we are able to mesh with the Mugnier-Barton forces."

"Regardless, we need to be appreciative of all those old military vehicles their boys kept stored, full of gas, and in good working order," Noble said. "That insight on Mugnier's part was genius. We need to do this right. Y'all Qaeda from Boyle City won't give us a second chance to ambush them."

Maguire nodded. "Let's do what we can to confirm this, and then get to work."

***

Prescott's eyes snapped open at the sound of pounding on her door. She was halfway up in bed when the door opened, and a head came into view.

"Alert, Staff Sergeant! Not a drill, full battle-rattle, per Sergeant Maguire," the woman called out, then departed as suddenly as she had come.

"Well, that escalated quickly," Prescott mumbled. She automatically started dressing, even as she heard the sound of boots running out of the building. She dressed quickly, ticking off the combat gear she would need from the list burned into her brain. Methodical but quick, she pulled on her ballistic vest, then her modular vest with extra ammo magazines, water, first aid packet, and compass. Once everything was snapped into place, she jumped up and down twice, settling the gear. She grabbed her helmet with its night vision goggles with one hand and her rifle with the other.

Breathing hard, Prescott arrived at the unit briefing room and dropped herself into a free chair. She pulled out her canteen, twisted open the cap, and sucked down a small amount of water. Looking around at the assembled women, she made a mental note of who looked ready and who did not.

Cy crashed down in the seat next to her, gently cradling her sniper rifle. There was a half-smile on her face. "I think I just ruptured a lung or something."

"You and me both, Cy," Prescott admitted as she watched the rest of the unit, including cadre, arrive and close the doors after the last.

Maguire rapped her knuckles on the whiteboard to call the group to silence. Her burning eyes scanned the thirty-some women. All were dressed appropriately, weapons on hand. Everyone was passing around sticks of camo paint and applying the goop to their faces, ears, and necks.

"Team leaders!" Maguire barked.

"Alpha team, all present and accounted for," Jennings called out.

"Bravo team, all present and accounted for," Huddler said in a soft tone.

"Charlie and cadre, all present and accounted for," Bixby responded. "Vehicles juiced and ready," she continued. "By your watch, we go outside the wire in seven mikes."

Maguire nodded. "Five days ago, unconfirmed HUMINT alleged a possible attack on our supporting town will be originating from Boyle City. We sent an agent into Boyle City to confirm. Our intel confirmed that what's left of Boyle City is home to white supremacists. Intel also confirms that a former resident of Sanctuary is now in the company of said white supremacists. Sanctuary militia is in receipt of this information and is going to Plan Bravo. We will shortly board vehicles by team and convoy to our rally points, where we will link up with Recon elements.

"Alpha team, Boyle City is nine klicks from us. Boyle City is too big for us to enter before we reduce their numbers. We will go hunting six klicks out. We will take out as many of them as we can, then push their dwindled numbers towards Piedmont. Bravo team, you will link up with Recon Bravo, two klicks outside of town. You will defend the town of Piedmont from anyone who gets past Alpha. Piedmont has defenses and will coordinate with you. Charlie, you will have perhaps the hardest job. You *will* let the threat pass you. I don't want you to move until you get radio word that we aren't all dead. Once you get that word, you will enter Boyle City, identify and mark targets. Alpha will also break off and enter Boyle City."

Bixby nodded, her jaw muscles working overtime. "Roger that, Top."

"If we *aren't* all dead, we will link up with one Charlie team member, who will lead us in, and then, ladies, we will take out as many remaining targets as possible."

Bixby raised her hand, then pointed to her assistant squad leader. "Chance will be lead in."

Maguire took in deep breath. "Because there is a former Sanctuary resident apparently directing their attack, we are facing a situation where they know more about us than we do them. What they don't know is that we found out about their plan before they could execute it, and that works to our advantage. The former resident is Carrie." She continued smoothly, ignoring the roomful of baleful murmurs. "My ancestors took the head of their enemy, boiled the flesh off, dipped the skull in pewter and used it for drinking." Her voice hardened. "I want that cunt's head on my fecking desk. I *will* drink my Irish whiskey from her skull on every anniversary of this battle." The Irish brogue of her ancestors flowed without conscious thought.

"Team leaders, pick up your marked maps from Bixby," Maguire continued. "Militia has changed the sign/countersign for this mission. Militia sign is Airborne. Our countersign is Currahee. If anyone forgets that, I will kick your arse before we drop your corpse into the hole. Bixby, time?"

"Four mikes. Get your asses in gear to the vehicles. Team leaders, I have maps. Weapons check before you get onboard," Bixby ordered crisply, holding up marked envelopes for the team leaders. "Radio checks! Do not forget your radio checks," she called out. "Com up on the vehicles," she finished with a snap in her voice, and then she darted out the door.

Maguire allowed herself a brief smile, then slid the communication headset onto her head. Lastly, she donned her helmet and snugged it down. When she looked up, she saw

Prescott standing there.

"For Szabo and Jess," Prescott said quietly.

"For Szabo and the L.T.," Maguire agreed. "I put you on Charlie team as an advisor because that's where you belong. Big picture."

"You think I don't know that?" Prescott grinned. "See you in Boyle City. Don't be late."

"You sound like my ex-wife," Maguire shot back.

Prescott shook her head. "You just had to ruin it all by saying that, didn't you?" Then she dashed out the door.

Chapter Twenty-Three

Master Sergeant Lewis had her list in hand, and everything was moving along as she thought it should, with one hugely notable exception. The livestock department had all its shepherds moving in concert, calming the stubborn animals as they reluctantly went into the large cargo elevators. Each elevator could take a ton and a half, which was a lot of cow. Lewis smiled at the thought.

A runner whose nametag read "Radner" stopped and bent over in front of her, trying to calm her labored breathing. Lewis patted Radner's shoulder, letting her know she should take her time. Lewis flicked the mic of her com to activate it. "Lewis to Miller."

"Miller to Lewis. Go," came the answer.

"I have civilians wandering around. What gives? Over." she asked with all the patience in the world.

"Miller to Lewis. We are aware and trying to fix it. Continue yours. Over." The answer was relayed smoothly.

"Who are they? Over."

There was a brief moment of silence over her headset, then... "The Warrens faction. Over."

"Lewis, roger and out." She turned her attention to Radner. "What do you have for me?"

"All departments are ready for lockdown. I did a full run around. We're good, Massersergeant," Radner said.

"Good, except for civs not inside where they should be," Lewis groused.

Radner looked at her idol and grinned. "You trust me, Master Sergeant?"

Lewis's laugh was guttural. "What is that going to cost me?"

"A dinner with you." Radner's voice was cheeky and serious at the same time, and then she winked. "I have friends who can make those civs run." Her voice was musical, as she added, "C'mon, Lewis, walk on the dark side."

Lewis laughed full and hard. She took a breath and purred, "Oh, child, I *am* the dark side."

Radner sucked in air and her face beamed with a wide grin. "I know. That's why I said it. Count on it—the civs will be moving in less than five."

Lewis' expression turned serious. "We lock down in ten. No exceptions."

"It's a date." Radner flashed another grin before she dashed off.

Lewis shook her head and laughed. For the first time since the alert had sounded, she felt good. Life was looking up. She walked toward the temporary D-TOC headquarters, where she would await her next orders. Despite everything that was going on, the thing that stuck in her mind was that she was going to have to find out Radner's first name.

***

Despite the lingering pain in her rib area, Anna moved as quickly as she could. She managed to shove two gurneys over into the temporary medical wards. The surgical trays, such as they were, were in place and ready if needed. She had already checked the three triage rooms for cots, bandages, water, and IVs. The makeshift hospital was as ready as it could be.

Mr. Cameron stepped through the front door carrying a large box of rolled bandages. "Where do you want these?"

Anna pointed to her left, "Room two, on the counter to the right. Please take them out of the box and set them out horizontally," she barked. She began to walk away, stopped and turned back to face Mr. Cameron. "I'm sorry. That sounded rude."

"Nonsense," he said gruffly. "Sounds like you know what you're doing. Don't ever mistake having to give orders for being rude. If you had been rude, I'd be snapping back at you." He hefted the box a little higher and carried it into the room she had indicated.

"You mean that wasn't snapping?" she commented to herself in a low voice. "Wow. Good to know."

***

Lewis checked her watch and shook her head.

"Two minutes," came the voice over her radio. "Lockdown in two minutes."

Shit. Master Sergeant Lewis peered into the darkness one last time, then had no choice but to turn and start walking to the steel outer doors that would lock out everyone who had been too slow. She forced herself to keep moving forward instead of looking back.

The sound of heavy running footfalls and a muffled voice made her stop and look back. Two militia members were dragging the red-faced, gagged and bound Warrens woman between them, with Radner trailing behind them and losing distance, calling off the time.

"Go, go, go. One mike, thirty seconds! Move your asses!" Radner ground out sharply.

Lewis reached the door first. She shot a glance at the doorkeeper, who was waiting, fidgeting. The doorkeeper lifted her right wrist, tapped her watch, then flashed four fingers on one hand and five on the other. When the first three stragglers got close enough, Lewis stepped out and grabbed Warrens by the front of her shirt and yanked. With the added momentum, they all fell forward, past the threshold, just as the doors whined in warning and quickly began to close.

Lewis looked up from where she lay. Apparently realizing that she wasn't going to make it, Radner limped to a stop ten yards outside the threshold. Blood was running down her leg and into her boot, and she obviously had nothing left in her tank.

Radner's lips twitched into a weak smile. "Sorry I was late, Master Sergeant Lewis. Dinner's on me after this shit show is done. Watch that bitch. She bites."

The outer doors slid closed. A low alarm sounded, and a mechanical voice announced, "Thirty seconds to blast door closure. Thirty seconds to blast door closure."

The group scrambled to their feet, then grabbed their prisoner and dragged her beyond the threshold of the reinforced blast door. The prisoner and her two guards fell to ground, but Lewis managed to keep her feet as the doorkeeper followed them inside. Ten seconds later, the doors came together with a loud hiss, followed by a series of dull, mechanical thuds.

Lewis looked at the militia members, who were still breathing hard. "What the hell happened?"

"Master Sergeant, Private Kilts reporting. I request Military Police to take custody of this Papa Oscar Sierra. Rads caught her trying to open back gate 154, and we had to take her down. I wanted to kill the bitch, but Rads said it would be better to bring her in alive. And Rads is right—the fucking bitch bites. I think I need a rabies shot," Kilts rattled out, and then laid back, sucking in air. "Should have killed her," she wheezed. "Then Rads would have made it."

Lewis grabbed her hand mic. "Lewis to Miller. Over."

"Miller to Lewis. Go with your traffic."

"I need MPs at blast gate Charlie, and tell Medical that they have three incoming—two friendlies, one under guard. And tell Noble I damn well need to talk to her. Yesterday. Over."

"Roger. Stand by for confirmation. Over."

***

Jennings ducked around the corner of the building as a round buried itself in the brick by her head. She sucked in a deep breath and pushed on, following her Recon battle buddy, James Smythe, toward the danger. She sighted down the barrel of her M4 and shot off three rounds in the direction of incoming fire. She ducked lower, taking to heart the lessons she had learned. She slid to the ground and crawled forward, keeping Smythe in sight, though just barely. She saw him drop down on one knee.

She pushed to her feet, gulping in air as she rushed forward for about fifteen yards. Back down on one knee, she lifted her rifle and pounded out two three-round bursts. Then she was back up and moving forward during a break in enemy fire.

Above the other fire patterns, Jennings heard a single round and, in the blink of an eye, saw Smythe stutter step and fall, his gear scattering around him. She didn't hesitate. She slung her rifle on her back and dashed forward until she could reach out and grab the webbing gear at the back of his neck. Nearly dislocating her right shoulder in the process, Jennings pulled Smythe to the four-foot wall on their right. Protected by the wall, she dropped down and pulled him into her lap. She cradled his head and saw that he was exhaling blood out of a gaping hole in his neck.

Frantic, she reached into one of her utility pockets and yanked out a maximum absorbency sanitary napkin. She ripped it out of its packaging, unfolded it, and pressed it against his throat.

His legs thrashing against the wall, Smythe tried to speak and breathe at the same time, accomplishing neither. "Fu...sssss."

"Quit it, goddamn it!" Jennings tightened her hold around his body and leaned over him to adjust the pressure on the napkin.

"Shi.." Blood soaked the padding as Smythe tried to speak again.

She pressed harder, but it was no use. As she leaned closer to him, blood suddenly splattered her face and hair. Jennings was not prepared for him to just deflate in her arms. His blood dripped off her face and onto his chest, which did not rise again. For a long moment, she could only blink, then she looked at his face. Blue-green eyes flickered, and then went empty. She shook him twice, then realized what she was doing. He was gone.

Anger seared up in her from her boots to her head. Both hands wrapped around her helmet and she pulled it off and threw it in the direction of the enemy. In that moment, she absolutely lost her mind. Smythe had been an arrogant asshole, but he was *her* arrogant asshole. She moved him off her lap, then gently closed his eyelids.

"You fucking asshole, you weren't supposed to die on me," she choked out. "They're dead, Smythe, I'm going to fucking kill them all," she promised him in a hoarse whisper.

Jennings adjusted her vest gear and then fell to her chest and slowly slithered towards Smythe's sniper rifle. She wasn't as good as he was with the gun, but she was more than adequate. She would avenge her partner. Her fingers closed around his sniper rifle and pulled it close, then she rolled over and sucked in a hard breath.

***

Maguire watched through her scope as Jennings stood, head down, looking at the body of one of the Recon boys. When Jennings lifted her face to the sky, Maguire could clearly see the blood drying on her camo face paint. She couldn't hear the scream to the heavens, but she could see it, and a chill ran down her spine as her mind whispered, *Morrigan.*

***

Cy grinned as she settled herself in the bell spire of the church. She was exhausted, sore, and wired at the same time. It was the most alive and the most dead tired she'd ever felt in her life. Suddenly, there was a tap on the top of her headgear.

"Two at ten o'clock. Three meters apart," Sims murmured from behind his spotter scope. "Five hundred yards. Wind left to right, six miles per hour."

"Got 'em," she whispered back. She snugged her rifle butt against her shoulder and shifted her aim slightly until the crosshairs were set on the middle of the first target. "Extra magazine ready?" Cy asked quietly.

Sims grinned in the dark. "If I wasn't married, I'd ask you out. Magazine ready."

"If you weren't married, I'd ask your 'not wife' out." Cy

chuckled softly as she tracked her target. "Firing." She squeezed the trigger gently and absorbed the recoil through her body. The target vanished from her field of vision. She adjusted quickly. "Switching."

"Target moved position. Twelve o'clock. Same conditions." Sims sighted on the target to confirm and then moved the scope slightly.

"Firing." She repeated her series of actions. The target fell out of her vision. She dropped the empty magazine. "Reload." She held out her left hand and, without taking her eye off the scope, felt for the edge of the magazine Sims placed in her hand, reloaded, and let the bolt slide forward. Then she scanned for more targets.

Sims spat his dip. "Your girl, the one y'all are looking for, about five feet eight, shoulder length dark hair, right? Bitter expression?"

"Yep." Cy didn't take her eye off the scope, though not much was in her zone.

"Seven o'clock. Trying to be Zen with that crooked armed tree." His words were clipped with tension.

Cy scanned the area, pulled back from the scope, adjusted a knob with her left hand, and resettled. The view in her scope zoned in. "I'll be fucking damned. I only have a profile view, but I think that's her." She moved slightly. "Do me a favor. Can you put two rounds just to her left? I need her to move to the right just a touch."

He pulled his own rifle to his shoulder and shifted away from the scope. "To her left? Really?"

"Oh, yeah. I got something special for her. You ever see the movie *The Jackal?*"

Sims thought for a moment as he sighted. "Bruce Willis, right?"

"Yeah." Cy settled in and pulled her rifle in tight. "Bad guy shoots this female Russian, she's the good guy by the way, in the liver."

Sims spat once and eyed his scope. "So, your girl is a fuckhead, right?"

"Yep."

"Sounds good to me. I'm in." He lined up his shot. "Take her after my second shot."

Cy grunted agreement.

Sims squeezed the trigger, then took two slight breaths and squeezed again.

Cy watched Carrie flinch, then move. Her finger stroked the trigger. This time she watched as her target reacted, standing almost to full height, then folding in on herself and dropping to the ground. "Anything else moving?"

Sims scanned. "All of it is moving away from us. If I wasn't so secure with myself, I'd get a complex or something." He spat again.

"I can see that," Cy murmured. "I'd like to go say hi to Carrie. Wanna watch my six?"

"Don't have too much more planned today, so yeah." He grinned. "Good shots."

"I may have missed one," Cy admitted as she began feeling around for empty magazines.

"Yeah. Second shot, but you got the guy behind the original target, so, no harm, no foul."

"Thanks, Red," Cy whispered, then slithered backwards to get out of her partner's way.

***

Cy ambled up to Carrie with exactly zero sympathy in her. Her former ally still had enough energy to writhe in pain, her head and neck supported by the tree she had been trying to hide against.

"Bad day, *Captain of the Guard?*" Cy asked casually as she sank down to one knee, the butt of her rifle on the ground.

"Get me a fucking doctor," Carrie gritted through clenched teeth.

Cy slowly shook her head. "I'd like to, but they're all busy."

"A medic, a healer... Fuck, get me a candy striper," Carrie ordered.

Cy shrugged. "Fresh out. Sorry."

"Then what the fuck are you doing here?"

The satisfied grin that crossed Cy's lips was sinister and casual at the same time. "Checking my handiwork."

"*You* fucking shot me?" Carrie lurched upward, forgetting her pain until it drove her to fall sideways and crash heavily into the filthy slush.

"Yeah." Cy leaned forward a little. "Got this thing against treason, you know? Like, you'd be pissed if I sold you out or something like that. Kind of like you handing all our secrets to a fucking Nazi biker gang. Now, biker gang is bad enough, and Nazis are bad enough, but you had to find a Nazi biker gang. That's like a buy one, get one free thing, which in this case, gets you shot. You shouldn't have sold us out, Carrie."

Carrie tried to laugh, but it ended up as a cough. "You, too? Maguire got to you too?"

Cy shook her head. "You don't get it do you, Carrie?" She leaned in close and whispered into the woman's ear, "You remember Helen Phillips?"

Carrie shook her head. "Get me some fucking help."

"Helen was my girlfriend, until you and your friends constantly harassed her." Cy settled her butt on the ground and got comfortable. "She didn't even tell me about it while it was going on. She left me a note the night she left Sanctuary. Did you know she left Idaho? She probably died out there during the attack. And that bought you a bullet in the liver."

Realization crossed Carrie's face. "Revenge, then."

Cy shook her head. "Retribution. I was going to ask her to marry me. And now...well now, I kill people for a living."

Carrie coughed. "So that's my fault?" She tried to press harder against her wound.

"Sort of. You were the catalyst. Who knew I'd be good at killing people like you? So, thank you for letting me learn that."

Carrie squirmed in her position until her head rested against the tree. "Going to gloat now?"

"No. I'm going to watch you die," Cy answered simply.

Chapter Twenty-Four

William Owens, the former mayor of Boyle City, took a deep breath and then walked into his former office. He was met by two men in military uniforms, and Rachel Noble, whom he recognized. He cringed inwardly at the thought of her taking her pound of flesh. He had not been welcoming when she and her compound opened. In fact, he had passed along some of the nastier rumors that had popped up about the women who had taken up residence there.

"Have a seat, Mr. Owens. I'm General Barton, this is General Mugnier, and I believe you know Rachel." Barton waved Owens to sit, which he did rather tentatively. "Are you well enough to walk us through what's been going on here?"

Owens swallowed and nodded. "I am." He shifted his gaze to Rachel and nodded. "Ms. Noble." His voice was laced with what sounded like regret.

"Let's not go there, Owens. We both know your sentiments about me and mine." She shifted comfortably in her chair and stared at him. "Right now, we're fact finding. What happened, when, and how? Where are the rest of your citizens and, most importantly, who collaborated with the group our collective forces just kicked ass on?"

Owens shifted his gaze to the two men, in hopes they might help him out.

General Mugnier's expression hardened. "I lost two Recon Marines, Bill. Men I *personally* trained. What she said. Now."

Owens nodded in resignation and cleared his throat. "Most of the residents were okay after the initial attack. Lots of us have underground…not bunkers, but storage areas or cellars, because of tornados and the like."

"Bullshit." General Mugnier coughed. "I've been in the area for more years than you might have noticed. You all were building bunkers because a black man was president. I heard you talking in local diners, my wife went to your city meetings, my sons used to drink beer with your boys down on the river. I may have spent my career in a lot of places, but my people began here. They were local. That's why my family and I spent our leave time here, but none of you noticed us because when you take off the uniform you don't want to be noticed. You were hiding your guns because some idiot politicians convinced you *idiots* that the president was going to come and take your guns.

"I didn't always like or agree with that president, but I'll tell you this," the general continued, "he never bullshit me. When he was sending my boys into the shit, he told me it wasn't going to be a cakewalk, and he never claimed victory when there was none." Mugnier took in a deep breath. "Now, get to the truth or get out of my sight."

Owens crumpled back into his seat. "After the main attack, we all took care of each other, getting information from the ham radio operators out there. About three weeks, maybe a month after the main attack, the Knights of White Heritage arrived. They brought in food, and some intel about the attacks."

Barton leaned forward. "What kind of intel?" he snapped.

"I don't know all of it. The city planner told us that the attacks came from the anti-fas and the Clinton backers." He looked up at the ceiling. "That bullshit, I didn't believe."

"What is the name of the city planner?" Barton brought up his notebook.

"Dennison. George Dennison. I haven't seen him since I was thrown into the cell," Owens answered. "I know he spent a lot of time with the Knights." He licked his lips. "May…may I have a glass of water?"

Rachel pushed her chair back from the table. "We'll take ten." She stood and started to walk away, then stopped and looked at Owen. "When was the last time you were fed?"

Owens blinked repeatedly. He truly didn't know. "What day is it?"

"Thursday," General Mugnier answered in a softened voice.

"They fed me three days ago," Owens said.

Rachel blinked away tears that unexpectedly formed. "We'll take half an hour. I hope sandwiches are okay for you. We aren't set up for much more than that."

Owens dropped his head. "I don't want to be a bother."

"It's not a bother, Mr. Owens," Rachel assured him. "Despite our differences, I don't want you in any further misery. I'll send Corporal Chance to take you to the temporary kitchen. Please eat, but don't overdo it," she finished, then walked out the door.

Owens turned to look at the generals. "I don't understand."

"She might be a hard ass, and she might on occasion piss you off to no end, but she is one of the most humane people I've ever known." General Mugnier sighed. "She's probably kicking herself right now for not figuring out earlier that you hadn't eaten in days."

Owens blinked repeatedly, obviously confused. "But that's not her job."

"Try and tell *her* that," General Barton said quietly.

***

Jennings and Mike Bradford, her newly issued Recon counterpart, entered the warehouse with the Boyle City school district manager, Amy Chorinos. The uniformed personnel gently pushed the civilian to the rear as they entered with weapons up. Once they had methodically cleared the area, they waved her in.

"What have we got in here?" Bradford had a deep baritone voice that did not fit with his slight stature.

"School uniforms, books, supplies, and ROTC stuff." Chorinos pulled her coat more tightly around her body. "Normally we have some heat going."

"No worries." Bradford glanced at Jennings. "What are

we looking for?"

Jennings shrugged. "Not a clue. The people in charge want an inventory of everything." She turned and looked at Chorinos. "You got paperwork?"

Chorinos rolled her eyes. "I've got paperwork for days— stuff that was bought at wholesale prices, on sale, or even just a screwed-up ROTC order. Talk about a waste of money. Frigging stupid berets that weren't the right style. About never heard the end of that one."

Jennings nearly ran into the wall as she turned to look at Chorinos. "Stop right there. Say again?"

"Yeah." Chorinos looked sideways at Jennings. "We had a new purchasing officer. The city has five high schools, almost six thousand students. Of that number, there are nearly twelve hundred student JROTC cadets. He found a sale on the berets, and ordered and paid for them. Keep in mind, he had no military experience. He bought British military berets in brownish khaki for every JROTC cadet."

"How does that happen?" Bradford grumbled. "I'm a Marine, and even *I* know that Army wears black berets."

Chorinos snickered. "His nephew was on the drill team, and they liked the new brown berets. He added one and one, and came up with fifty. So...there we are. According to him, they were on sale. The district JROTC commander imploded and chewed his ass. The district never got its money back. And then the shit hit the fan."

A grin covered Jennings face. "Miss Chorinos, I think that we might be able to come to a deal on those misbegotten berets."

Chorinos turned, her expression incredulous. "You can't be serious."

"You haven't met my commander." Jennings laughed for real for the first time in more than twenty-four hours. "Please show me these mistakes."

***

Her normally robust coloring draining to ash, Delores

Warrens stared at Noble. "You're sure it was *my* Brittany who defected and helped organize the attack against Sanctuary?" Noble nodded. "*My* daughter joined a biker gang that wanted to kill us all?" Delores' tone was breathless with disbelief.

Recognizing the woman's distress, Noble gave her a moment before continuing. "Honestly, Delores, Brittany has been a pain in my ass ever since you chose to stay in Piedmont and sent her to stay with us as your representative. She questioned everything I did, demeaned pretty much everything I said, and openly disrespected me by challenging nearly all of my instructions and orders. She resented not being in charge. This may shock you, but believe me when I tell you, her most recent actions sound just like what I am used to seeing from her.

"Your daughter had a consensual relationship with Carrie. We have eyewitness testimony from one of our counter intelligence agents who saw Carrie make contact with your daughter hours after Carrie attacked two women from Sanctuary and then ran. Mind you, this contact was well away from Sanctuary. Your daughter then had contact with four other women who used to be under Carrie's command. On the night of the attack, those women were also caught trying to allow the enemy entry to Sanctuary. Your daughter was observed by militia trooper Radner attempting to open one of the back gates. Upon being discovered, your daughter bit Trooper Radner and two other militia troopers.

"My intel said their intention was to take over Sanctuary and its resources, which would require killing or capturing any opposition. Since Brittany was well aware of what our residents were trained for, and what we had in supply and storage, I can't imagine she or her gang had any plans for sharing the power or space with us.

"I just don't understand this." Delores blinked back tears. "What happens now?"

"Brittany will have to go before a tribunal, and no, I will not be on the tribunal. We will blind-pick the panel. and they will make the final decision." Noble's voice was laced with exhaustion. "You may choose any attorney from those among our residents."

"Thank you, Rachel. You could have just summarily..." Warrens' voice failed her.

"As creator of Sanctuary, I have to make a lot of the decisions on my own, without the council's approval. This, however, is very different. The actions of a few are affecting the many." She took a sip of hot tea. "In this case, the representatives of the many *have* to make this decision."

***

Cy braced her back against the wall of the high school and raised her rifle. With a nod of her head, she signaled to Sims that she was ready.

He kicked in the door and dropped to the ground, rifle up, sweeping left and right. Nothing moved in his view. "Go," he shouted.

Without a moment's thought, Cy proceeded past him, sweeping left and right with her weapon. She nearly pulled the trigger when she caught sight of something on her left periphery, but in a second recognized it as biology class skeleton. "Clear," she shouted.

"Clear," Sims confirmed. He relaxed and progressed further into the room. "Don't you just love our job?" He turned his head and spat some dip into the trashcan.

"That's what I love about you, Sims." She grinned. "You might spit, but you're polite about it."

"That's my wife's fault." Sims smiled back at her. "And what I like about you is that you know your shit. This is the last room, right?"

She nodded. "Call it in on the radio. We can go down and grab some chow and downtime."

"Sounds good."

Cy didn't move. She was still looking at the skeleton. "Hey, Red, wanna help me take that skull off?"

"Okay, but why?"

"Why?" She stepped back and looked at the materials in

the Biology classroom. "I guess the answer is that I'm going to make my Top Sergeant a fucking legend."

Sims snorted. "Your Top Kick is *already* a fucking legend."

"Yeah." She grinned. "But with what I have in mind, no one will ever question it." She proceeded to tell him about Maguire's pre-battle speech and her own plan.

Sims laughed out loud. "Fuck it. I'm in. But if anyone asks, I was on guard duty."

CHAPTER TWENTY-FIVE

Nearly three hundred Sanctuary residents stood in the sharp chill of mid-morning, waiting. Only those who were elsewhere on duty were not in attendance. Militia members stood in formation, facing the open area used for Sanctuary bell calls. Small groups of people murmured together in quiet, respectful tones.

Anna and Angel stood in silence near the front of the civilian gathering. The crowd hushed as Rachel Noble and the department heads walked onto the field, followed by Master Sergeant Lewis and three volunteers from the Logistics department, each of whom carried a small box. They stopped in the middle of the field near a small speaker. An audio-visual technician stepped forward and clipped a microphone to Noble's lapel, then plugged the attached cord into an audio pack belted around her coat.

There was a respectful silence as the surviving members of the newest commando class marched in formation to stand next to the militia. Their instructors stood by at attention.

From the far edge of the field, the commandos marched into view led by Maguire in her bottle green beret. As they reached the center of the field, everyone in attendance could see that their uniforms were pressed and their boots highly shined. They exuded an aura of pride. The entire group didn't march so much as they strutted, within regulations.

"Unit, halt," Maguire called out. The commandos took one additional step, and then stopped in place as one. "Right, Face." The commandos turned to their right as one. Maguire took two steps back. "Open ranks, March."

The first row took one step forward, the middle row stood fast, and the third row took one step back. "Stand at,

Ease." The commandos shifted their stance—feet shoulder width apart, hands placed behind their backs, right over left, bodies slightly relaxed. "Cadre. Post." Commando instructors positioned by the commando cadets now joined the commando formation, creating a new row.

Maguire turned on her heel to face Noble and the crowd. "Unit, Atten-tion."

The commandos dropped their arms to their sides, thumbs perfectly aligned with the seams of their BDU pants. Their heels came together with a snap, their feet at a forty-five-degree angle, and they looked directly ahead. Maguire executed an about face and snapped to attention as Noble stepped forward to address the gathering.

"First, I would like to acknowledge our militia. When we have decided on an appropriate emblem for your unit, there will be a ceremony to honor your bravery, as well." Rachel Noble paused a moment to let that sink in. "Today we recognize these women, and the five who are still in the infirmary." Noble took a breath as she waited for the applause to die down. "Sergeant Maguire has created a commando school that has incredibly high standards, demanding every ounce of not only effort, but will. The excellence of this commando school was demonstrated here, in town, and in Boyle City." She pointed at the cadets. "This most recent class is beginning its third week of training. These cadets are the seventeen survivors of an initial corps of twenty-five." Tears filled many eyes that shifted to look at the young fighters, then fixed again on Noble.

"I've heard some complaints about our joining forces with Generals Mugnier and Barton. Their Recon force sustained two killed in action and three wounded. They bled with us and for us." She looked out across the gathering. "The founding principle of Sanctuary will not be changed—men will not live at Sanctuary. But Sanctuary also will not hide its head in the sand. We must acknowledge the forces that have gathered to destroy this country and this world, and what it will take to defeat them. We will not isolate ourselves from our allies, or from victims of this unmitigated crime. And we will carry our share, and sometimes more than our share, of responsibility for whatever it takes for all to survive and thrive." Noble turned and motioned for Maguire to join her.

Maguire stepped forward and was wired up by the audio-visual tech, then she cleared her throat. "I'm not much for public speaking, so I'll make this short.

"These women behind me are Sanctuary commandos. Today they will trade their soft patrol caps for a symbol long associated with commandos, the beret." She flashed a sly grin before turning to the commandos. "You will thank Mrs. James and her brigade of needle wielding companions." She took some satisfaction from her soldiers' confused expressions, then turned back to the assembly. "We Celts have a goddess of war. Her name is Morrigan, and she is symbolized by the raven." Maguire paused. "She leads only those *worthy* to be her warriors. These women are the first, but will not be the last, of this commando unit, now and forever to be known as Morrigan.

"You will recognize them by the khaki beret and the green raven on the front. The raven will be looking to the commando's left. Our Morrigan commandos will give all they have for the protection of others, just like the warriors who were favored by the goddess Morrigan." She took a breath and released it slowly. "Ms. Noble, if you would." Maguire stepped back and unplugged her microphone from the wire.

Noble stepped up to the first squad leader, took a rolled beret from a box, and handed it to the soldier. She waited as the woman pulled off her soft patrol cap and stashed it in her cargo pocket, slid the beret into place, the raven directly over her left eye, and then snapped to attention.

The ceremony took forty-five minutes, as Noble spoke a few words to each Morrigan. When it ended, every member of the Morrigan had her beret in place. Maguire called the Morrigan to Parade Rest, and then walked back up to the PA system and plugged in her microphone.

"For those of you who don't know, I currently wear the beret of the Fianóglach, the Army Ranger Wing of the Irish Defense Forces. Commandos, I am very proud of this beret."

Master Sergeant Lewis stepped up to her side and reached into the box held by one of the volunteers.

Maguire took off her Fianóglach beret, rolled it, and slid it into the right cargo pocket of her uniform. She accepted a khaki beret from Lewis and settled it on her head. "Fianóglach is my past. Morrigan is my present and my future." Maguire directed her gaze across the crowd. "Every future cadet who passes the Morrigan course will have earned the right to bear the name. The Morrigan will outlive all of us, and we will be better for them."

***

Angel noticed Lisa sitting away from the rest of the Morrigan, just at the edge of the firelight, a bottle of beer in her hand and, oddly, the new beret sitting at her side instead of on her head. Trying not to seem as if she was deliberately going there, she slowly made her way in Lisa's direction. Angel slid in next to Jennings and scooted down until her back was against the log, mirroring the older woman's position.

"What's up?" Jennings voice sounded tired.

Angel jutted her chin in the direction of the fire. "Kind of not my thing."

"You don't like hanging out with us?" Jennings's teasing was halfhearted at best.

Angel smiled. "Hanging out is okay. I just…they're talking about our people who got hurt and who got killed." She took a deep breath. "And they're talking about shooting and killing people."

"Yeah, I know. It's not easy, Angel." She looked up at the dark sky. "You sign up for this, and the training about grinds you into hamburger. Then you have to use your training, and it's your battle buddy who gets turned into hamburger. You have to listen to his last breath. And then you get pissed and kill those assholes who killed him and are trying to kill you."

"How do you do it?" Angel asked softly, turning her eyes to the Morrigan who were by the firelight.

"I don't know," Jennings answered honestly. "I'm over here because I don't know." She took a deep breath and let it out. "I don't know if I can continue to kill people."

"If you want, I can go," Angel offered reluctantly.

"Nah, you're good. I might not be good company."

"It's okay. I like being with you guys."

Jennings managed a small smile. "Even when we're being downers?"

Angel considered for a brief moment. "I guess nobody can be up all the time, right?" She shifted against the log. "I'm not always happy, but lots of times I am. It's the same kind of thing, right?" She hesitated, then continued. "It's like when I remember my mom. There were a lot of bad times, and those don't make me happy. But once in a while, I remember something good that she said or did, and I'm happy, because it was a happy moment. Could it be like that?"

Jennings nodded. "It could be like that," she agreed, her heart a bit lighter. "I don't know why it bugs me so much. I mean Smythe was an asshole most of the time."

Angel shrugged. "But he was your battle buddy, right? He had your back."

"Yeah. I don't have a clue why I feel this way. I don't like feeling this way."

"She was supposed to be my mom forever. If I could, I'd go back in time and kill the guy who raped her. That started it for my mom. Maybe Smythe dying just started it for you?"

Jennings turned her gaze to Angel. "You're kind of smart for a teenager."

"I wouldn't go that far." Angel's smile began timidly, but grew when Jennings winked at her.

***

Maguire unlocked the door to her office and entered, took off her new beret and tossed it onto her desk. She pulled her Fianóglach beret out of her cargo pocket and turned to place it on the top shelf of her bookcase. And froze.

On the center shelf, in the midst of her many field manuals, was a dull silver skull. It looked human, and a cruel smile twisted Maguire's lips.

"Well now, no one told me it was Christmas," she said aloud as she took a step forward to examine the gift. The metal coating certainly looked like pewter. She picked up the skull and turned it upside down. She felt a flash of satisfaction when she saw Carrie's name written in block letters alongside a military date. "I can only think of one wee bastard who'd do this." Her grin morphed into something genuine. "We need to put you someplace you can be seen," Maguire said to the skull. "Jaysus, I'm losing my feckin' mind." She laughed and shook her head.

***

Noble blinked repeatedly. "You have what?"

General Mugnier's smile stopped just short of being smug. "Hybrid vehicles— six SUVs and two mid-size sedans." Noble started to speak, but Mugnier held up his hand. "We didn't want to say anything until we had a fix for the loss of electricity caused by the EMPs. We managed to rig solar panels onto the vehicles. It took longer than expected to rig and test, but we are ninety percent certain this system will work."

Noble leaned back in her chair, astounded. "I thought you just had those old, gas powered Army Jeeps. This will make a huge difference in getting the team to Cheyenne Mountain."

Mugnier shook his head. "I don't know that we can get the team that far, but we can get them to Lehi a hell of a lot faster than we thought. After that, they'll need to rely on the same ingenuity and endurance it took Maguire's group to get here."

Nobel mulled over the possibilities, then said, "Before the world went to hell, Prescott worked on a prototype for DoD along these lines. I just don't know if we'll have the time to do a full reconfigure."

A frown creased Mugnier's brow. "Something you need

to update us on?"

Noble shook her head. "No, we're still on the same timeline. I'm just feeling a little stressed."

Barton stifled a snort. "Can't imagine why. It's not like we've got to save the world or anything."

Mugnier turned to his second in command. "Brendon, why do I keep you around?"

"Comic relief, Sir. I was top of my sarcasm class at the Point," Barton answered smoothly with a straight face.

"Rachel," the general turned back to Noble, "get with Prescott and see what we can reasonably expect to accomplish within our available timeframe. I'm getting feedback from Kimbrough regarding teamwork, and it looks good. Our strike team is back to pre-Boyle City levels. They're working together better than I could have hoped."

"I'm sorry about your casualties." Remorse laced Noble's voice.

"They were good men, and they volunteered." Mugnier swallowed hard as he looked out his office window towards the woods that contained the cemetery. "I visit them every day. They will not be forgotten." He shifted his gaze back to Noble. "An action report on Boyle City will be ready for you before you leave. I have a full platoon of scouts still out looking for the neo-Nazis that managed to get away during the firefight."

"Let us know when you find them. Morrigan will be happy to bring some firepower, should you request assistance."

"I will. Now, would you like to see our vehicles?" Mugnier asked with barely suppressed excitement.

This time Noble's smile was full and wide. "Lead the way, Al."

***

Prescott dropped the hood of the large vehicle she had just finished inspecting. She looked at Noble. "We can tie it all together." She jumped off the bumper and hurried back to a battered laptop computer affixed to a rusted iron stand in the motor pool in Mugnier's and Barton's camp. She tapped the keys at lightning speed. "Szab, you fucking genius wench, I wish you were here." She wiped away sudden tears. "You'd love this challenge, my friend. I'm going to do this in your honor." She gazed up. "Yeah, yeah, you're agnostic. Me? I'm a failed believer. I know you've got my six." Her eyes snapped to Noble. "I'm going to need some shit you might not have. And a team of Bright Betties."

"I have no idea what you just said, but we will find what you need," Noble promised.

"Someone has to have a math genius." Prescott bounced back and forth between the computer and the vehicles. "I need someone who can do the math I can't. Okay, eight vehicles of differing classes..." She did some calculations in her head on the fly. "I need a mile and a half, make that two miles, of wire. I'll get you the specs. Gas..." Again she did the math in her head. "Two five-gallon cans for the sedans, three five gallons for the SUV hybrids. We can use siphon pumps. They can all be accessed on the fly."

Noble blinked. "Did you take meth this morning?"

"Not available with pancakes in the chow hall," Prescott shot back. She lifted her head and stared at her sometimes lover. "*THIS* is what I do, Rachel. I was once a soldier and that was fine, but tinkering on something like this is what I was truly born for. God, I wish Szab was here for this." This time her grin was without sadness. "She taught me how to do this right."

"You seem so sure," Noble said softly.

"Because she taught me how to do this. I didn't know shit 'til Szab forced me to learn."

"Get us those specs and we'll get you what you need," Noble promised.

"Thank you, Rachel." Prescott didn't look up from the laptop. "Main battery line to the..."

Noble walked away without listening to the rest. She was out of her element and she knew it.

CHAPtER TWENty-SIX

Morrigan and Recon formed up on Maguire's command, and then Maguire rattled out instructions quickly and clearly. "Heavy gear goes in the SUV cargo areas; action packs go on your person. We will be driving during hours of darkness, under blackout conditions. Helmets and seatbelts, children. This will not be a cakewalk. There is snow and ice, and we will be going slow. Map says it's four hundred miles to Lehi. Expect three nights travel. We will stop during daylight and wait it out. We will go with fifty-fifty security. I hope you got enough sleep, children, because from here on out, rest is going to be a rare commodity. Squad leaders, get them ready and get them loaded. We go outside the wire in an hour. On the dot. Dismissed."

The unit immediately departed the formation area to gather their gear. Maguire watched them go, dread and confidence warring inside her. She turned on her heel and saw Anna and Angel standing nearby. "You two following me?" she teased.

Angel nodded vigorously. "I have been waiting for you to leave so I can take your tent."

"Nice try, kid, but that tent is going back to Morrigan cadre."

"It was worth a shot." Angel's mischievous grin faded. "I'll keep out of trouble."

"Noble made you promise that, didn't she?" Maguire's voice contained a hint of both laughter and compassion. Angel reluctantly nodded. "Good. Keep out of trouble, keep working with Morrigan, and pay attention to what is going on around you."

Angel snapped to attention. "The Goddess' Chosen," she

barked. It was the Morrigan motto.

Anna stepped forward and wrapped her arms around Maguire. "Mags, I'm going to miss you. Again." She closed her eyes.

Maguire hugged her tightly her return. "It won't be for long. You and Doc will be following soon enough. Make sure Prescott keeps working on the vehicle re-fits. You know how she likes to drag her feet."

Anna nodded and sniffled, "I will." She stepped back from Maguire and gazed at her sadly. "Is it always going to be like this, Mags?"

Maguire searched for the right words. "For a while, I think it will. Right now, we have to plan, pre-position, dig in, pull intel. After that, we'll have to fight again. I wish I could tell you when this shite might end, but I can't," she said honestly. "I'd love to be able to just sit back, read a book, and drink good Irish whiskey all day long. That's on hold." She looked directly into Anna's eyes. "I hope that someday we can just rest."

***

Bixby blinked behind her night vision goggles. Constant staring and green hued vision mingling with the cold air made her eyeballs feel like broken glass was living under her eyelids. She blinked again and touched her throat mic. "Alpha Actual, Charlie One, over," she murmured.

"Charlie One, go," Maguire replied softly.

"Alpha Actual, we are clear to target." She pointed the barrel of her rifle in the general direction of the location they wanted to get to. "Be advised, serious snow cover. If anyone's looking, they will see our prints. Over." Bixby propped her body against the corner of a burned-out brick building. A low chuckle came through her earpiece.

"Charlie One, roger that. Good thing I'm a witch; I brought a broom. Over."

"Didn't think to bring any rum-laced hot chocolate, did you? Over."

"Charlie One, sorry, no Jamaican Brown Cow. Next

time. Over."

"Alpha Actual, I'll add it to what you've promised me." Bixby scanned to her left and right, then up in the reverse direction. "Got an ETA for me? Over."

"Charlie One, seven mikes or less. Over," came the answer from Maguire.

"Roger. Charlie One, station keeping. Give me a heads up when you get close, so I don't shoot you. Over."

"Charlie One, roger that," Maguire promised. "Out."

***

Holding a medium bristle, long handled broom, Maguire stepped out of the former big box store and marched through the ice and snow to Jennings. "Hold this." She passed the broom off to her teammate and tugged the local city street map out of her coat and opened it, then refolding it until she had the correct section in view. For very long moments, she stared at every inch of it.

"What are you doing?" Jennings asked, leaning against a wall but still alert to everything around her.

"I'm staring at a map until my eyes bleed," Maguire answered. "It was recommended to me a lifetime ago." A tinge of emotion crept into Maguire's voice, and she clamped down hard on the memory. "Oddly enough, it works. I don't want to have to refer to a map in the middle of shit hitting the fan."

Jennings grinned despite the cold. "Sounds like good advice. Think we can move sometime soon?"

"Two mikes, Jennings, two mikes. We can double-time for five mikes or less and still make time." Maguire didn't exactly snap, but her tone was sharp.

Jennings nodded. "Roger that. Double time."

Maguire reached into her jacket and tapped the channel patch. "Alpha Actual to all elements, remain under cover. Alpha Actual moving out in less than two mikes. Will advise soon. Out." She tapped the channel button back to the previous setting. "Charlie One, Alpha Actual moving now.

Over."

***

Bixby touched her throat mic. "Roger." Continuing to surveil her area of responsibility, she spared a moment to will warmth into her body. For long minutes she looked forward, left and right, and up and down. Her night vision goggles let her see that her area was clear. It was a relief.

***

"Coming in," Maguire huffed into her throat mic, even as she started moving backwards quickly. "Charlie One, move up. Jennings is in the middle and I have clean up. Over." As she raced backwards, she swept snow left and right with the broom, covering their footsteps.

Bixby shifted up and forward. "Moving." She scanned her immediate area as she combat-walked to the target building, highly aware of the tightly packed ice and snow crunching under her boots.

The abandoned bi-level lodge wasn't exactly in the middle of nowhere, but it was far enough from any occupied areas that it would not garner unwanted attention. Tucked deep into a mountain recess, it had once been a retreat for people of the arts before it became a popular location for corporate team-building retreats. Now it was just another heavily vandalized structure. Off the beaten path, it was perfect for their shelter and makeshift HQ to regroup and re-energize, if their intel was accurate.

As Bixby neared the building, her newly honed instincts took over—assessing the scents behind the natural elements in the air and the sounds beyond the accustomed noises of the mountain. She inched closer to what looked as if it had been the employee entrance to a quaint café that once served the lodge guests. Stopping outside the door, Bixby flattened herself against the exterior wall and took shallow breaths. When she heard nothing suspicious, she cautiously eased the battered door inward.

"I'm in. Over," Bixby whispered into her throat com.

"Roger that," Maguire answered just as quietly. "I've located an office in the lobby behind the registration counter. Meet me there. Looks to be a back way through the kitchen so that you won't be exposed. Let's find our packages and secure this site. Over."

***

Walking point was a stress-inducing nightmare in the best of situations. Switching out from time to time eased the stress. Maguire and Bixby switched positions seamlessly without speaking. The carpet was cold enough to crunch under their feet, and the sound added to the eerie feeling of the cavernous, empty lobby.

"Our contact should be on the second floor in the gym area," Maguire relayed quietly as she scanned the lobby.

"Stairwell?" Bixby asked.

"Yeah," Maguire agreed. "This is definitely getting on my nerves."

"Hair on the back of my neck is going crazy in a way that has zero to do with the fact that it's make-my-face-hurt-cold. Over," Jennings murmured in their ears as they cleared the corner to her left.

"Welcome to the sexy life of an operator." Maguire grinned and pressed her mic button. "Jennings, your twenty? Over."

"South wing, second level, heading your way. Out," came the reply.

It took Maguire and Bixby ten minutes in total to find the stairwell door and climb the steps to the second level. They entered the corridor and then fanned out to take a look around. The level was one wide hallway with tagged, damaged Plexiglas walls surrounding the gym area. The hallway led to what was once the outdoor pool.

"Birds of a feather."

The young male voice came from somewhere within the gym, but the speaker was well concealed.

"Gather no moss." Bixby gave the countersign. "Who picks these signs, countersigns?"

"I think Angel is a Boondock Saints fan," Jennings answered, joining them in the open.

"Was that *in* the movie??

"I think it's the sentiment," Maguire answered, her rifle pointed in the direction from which the voice had come. "You inside, step out, hands up high. I don't think I need to add the 'no sudden moves' part, right?"

"No, no need. I'm coming out now." A moment later, an extremely thin figure emerged from cover and into the hallway, his hands comically high. He halted in front of the three women.

A youthful Ichabod Crane came to Maguire's mind.

"I'm Hobbs. I'm not armed, but I do have to tell you that we're on a little bit of a deadline here."

Maguire arched an eyebrow. "Deadline?"

"Yeah. The Powers-That-Be have an IR drone that consistently does a nightly fly-over scan," he warned. "It's like clockwork."

Maguire was surprised by the information, but maintained a neutral expression. "How much time?"

"It'll be back overhead in about twelve minutes. That's why we gave you the instructions that we did." He shuffled his feet. "Mage and CinC are already inside the bubble."

"That would be your hacker friends?" Maguire questioned. "And put your hands down."

He followed directions so quickly that it looked as if strings holding them up had been cut. "Yeah. We've got to move it, otherwise they'll find our heat signature, and I seriously *do not* want to find out the hard way what comes after that."

"About your instructions—how do I know the rest of my team is going to be safe?"

"The drone has a set path. It never varies. The car dealership we sent them to is not in its prescribed path. Even if it was, the dealership has an aluminum-lined storm shelter. As long as your people follow their instructions, they'll be fine. If you're cool with it, can we please get under some cover now?" His tone indicated that he was on the edge of panic.

"Lead the way, Hobbs." Maguire made the order sound like a request.

He led them to the snow-covered basin of the outdoor pool, where an oversized metal ball sat on a low concrete pedestal at each corner. Hobbs went to the corner at the far right end, where he pulled open a hatch door and gestured them inside. "We're safe in here," he promised.

Bixby eyed it suspiciously. "In that?"

"Yeah. Serious, dudes, we have to get inside."

"In," Maguire ordered, then led the way. It took her a moment to figure out how to move in the sphere, but she managed to not snag her weapon or gear on the seats inside the space. "It's a tsunami ball," she said, eyeballing the two men already inside. Both were wrapped in blankets. "Hello, gentlemen. Thanks for the accommodations."

Following Hobbs, Bixby and Jennings managed to enter the ball without incurring any physical harm.

Maguire took a few moments to remove her helmet and store her gear under the seat she'd chosen. She also sized up the two men she hadn't yet been introduced to. "I'm Maguire. These two are Bixby and Jennings."

"I'm CinC."

Maguire noted that he was stoutly shaped, with a nearly shaved head that sported a few centimeters of blond hair. She also guessed that shade had likely come from a bleach bottle.

"And I'm Mage."

Mage's head was the only part of him that Maguire could see. The rest of him was completely covered in a blanket. His shoulder length dark hair was greasy and unkempt. His eyes were bloodshot, his face lined with exhaustion.

"Sorry for the way I look, I'm fighting pneumonia or something." His voice sounded defeated.

Jennings reached into the light pack she'd dropped to the ground near her feet. "That would explain the request for these." She pulled out a bottle of antibiotics and held them out. "Doc said for you to take two every eight hours for the first twenty-four, then one every eight hours until the bottle's gone."

Mage slowly reached a hand out from his cocoon and grasped the bottle. His eyes closed for a moment as he rattled the pills. "Thank you, so much." There was relief in his voice as he opened the bottle and fished out two tablets.

CinC passed a bottle of water over to his companion, and Mage quickly swallowed the medication.

Bixby nodded at CinC. "You look familiar."

"Are you— or were you— law enforcement?" CinC asked.

"U.S. Marshal for about ten months before I joined Sanctuary. A year later, the shit hit the fan. Before that, Army for what seemed like forever," she answered.

"My hacker handle was CinCPactwo," he admitted.

Bixby blinked. "You died in prison."

"So they tell me." His smile was wan.

"I'm confused here," Maguire interrupted.

CinC shifted in his seat to look at her. "Do you remember the hacking incident about ten years ago—four banks, two electrical grids, and a supposedly hack-proof defense contractor?"

"No, but I was relatively busy out of the country," she admitted with a tight smile.

He nodded. "I did that. And got caught. I was in federal lock up until about three years ago. A dude named Segundo asked me if I wanted out of prison." He shook his head. "Like I was going to say no."

"I did those hacks as a challenge. Unfortunately for me, some people have no sense of humor. Josiah Franklin really didn't like that someone had found out about his back-door deals with the off-shore financial world. Evidence got sealed, I got a closed trial, and my dad got railroaded. Guilt by association. 'National Security' reasons. Only law enforcement would know my face, and only if they were around when I 'died'."

"Your dad was a rear admiral, upper half, right? A two star?" Bixby leaned back into her seat. "These chairs are actually kind of comfortable," she said with a grin.

"Pretty much the only comfort lately," Hobbs muttered. "We've been hiding in different places around the city for the last six weeks. There has been a lot of organized movement, but no uniforms. It seems to be small communities moving south. Well-armed and pretty fucking brutal. We watched one group stone a guy to death. We were hiding on the upper floor of the Adobe building." He shuddered. "I'm glad you all are here, and that we're leaving with you."

There was silence as CinC leaned over and lit a candle, then placed it between three cinder blocks centered in the ball. He carefully settled a ceramic flower pot over the candle, then looked at Bixby. "My dad's career was shit-canned. He had nothing to do with my hacking; he didn't even know about it. Hell, I was at Cal Poly, Dad was at Pearl." He let out a harsh breath. "I was a stupid kid. I really didn't set out to find what I found."

"So Franklin buried you and your family," Maguire summed up. "Hobbs, how'd you get into this?"

"Just lucky? Unlucky?" He shrugged. "I don't know."

Jennings cleared her throat. "I'm just wondering why we're in a metal ball with an IR drone flying around outside."

Mage tapped the frame near his head. "Aluminum body with insulation. IR can't see through aluminum. Once upon a time, Lehi was the tech Midwest's answer to Silicon Valley— mostly glass faced skyscrapers or old ass buildings, building materials IR can see through. As long we don't get this thing overheated, we're safe."

Maguire laughed softly until she became aware of five sets of eyes staring at her. She shrugged. "Tsunami balls in Utah. Struck me as funny."

"Well, thank God for an eccentric hotel owner. Dude had more money than sense. He wanted a designer lodge, so he built one where his friends could spend their money. Apparently he had one of these spheres at his mansion in Japan. He liked the functionality and he thought they looked artistic," Mage supplied.

"Dude, how do you even know that?" Hobbs asked.

"Framed magazine article in the main office." Mage

shrugged. "I got bored."

"I'm just glad it's warm enough in here that my face doesn't hurt like it did outside in the cold." Jennings stretched her legs out as far as space permitted.

Hobbs checked his watch. "We'll have to vent the heat when our sky is clear, but otherwise, we're safe. We'll need to get our computer gear before we leave."

"Where is it?" Bixby sneezed. "Sorry."

"Bless you. We hid our stuff in the server room. It seemed to make sense," CinC said. "We've been checking satellite imagery towards Cheyenne Mountain. The main roads are mostly clear until you get near Denver. We'll have to find a work-around. Then everything starts to thin out the closer we get to El Paso County."

"Can you mark it on a map when we have daylight?" Maguire asked, her eyes beginning to droop now that she wasn't freezing.

"We can," CinC answered. "What are the chances of getting to Cheyenne Mountain? Safely."

"We have a combined unit of Marine Recon and Fianóglach-trained commandos. You have a very high probability of getting there safely," Maguire promised. "Once we get to Interstate 70, I peel off to Dulce, New Mexico. The team will get you to Cheyenne Mountain."

"We can look at sat imagery in daylight for you," Mage said around a yawn. "Sorry. I'm wiped out."

Jennings leaned forward to stretch her back. "How long until we can leave?"

"Fly-overs are usually done by nine. So, like seven hours." Hobbs then gave them the bad news. "We'll have to shut down the heater soon. Don't want carbon monoxide poisoning. I have my watch alarm set for two hours, so at least we won't suffocate. We vent CO_2 through the night."

"Since we knew you were coming, we gave you our sleeping bags. They are under the seats. Might as well slide them on," Mage suggested as he closed his eyes. "I'm so fucking tired."

CHAPTER TWENTY-SEVEN

Maguire watched the convoy disappear from view before she took the turnoff to Interstate 70. Based on past consumption of gas and battery, she calculated that she had about seven hours of driving time available. That would take her to Pagosa Springs, Colorado. After that, she would be on foot for close to forty miles to get to Dulce, New Mexico.

A part of her was glad for the silence; a larger part of her missed the bickering and sometimes creative vocabulary of her strike team and the hackers. Those three had taken a great deal of getting used to. At least Mage was starting to look less like death warmed over. The drive from Lehi to Crescent Junction that typically took three-hours had taken them nearly eight, due to snow patches and driving in black-out mode. They still had nearly as much distance to travel as she did, but at least they had each other to rely on.

Maguire was well aware that she was totally on her own, but when it was time to go on foot, she would be able to move faster solo. It had taken her a very long time to understand and practice teamwork in the military. She was thankful that it hadn't affected her ability to function without a team.

***

Bixby checked her watch, adjusted her fucking, non-functional beret, and got up from her semi-relaxed position on the cold ground. She shrugged her gear into place then moved forward through the lines, using hand signals to direct the teams to their positions.

Other than the subtle noise of shifting bodies, there was

no sound. She had served with many different units in the Army for more than seventeen years, in peace and war, and now Armageddon. This was the unit Bixby was most proud of. They had been homegrown. From survivors to militia training to commando training, these women had not shirked. They had integrated well with General Mugnier's Recon boys and even bested them a time or two. They took tough training shit and then handed out a ration or five of shit with no apologies. They'd killed in defense and killed in offense. They were good. Not the best, but given time and more experience, they might well be the best someday.

Morrigan's own.

Bixby shook her head. *Damn that Maguire. Naming this commando unit after the Celt Goddess of War.* She smiled in the dark. Her own half Irish granny would have been proud of the name. And damn her if the name didn't fit.

By virtue of a night scope, Bixby had seen Jennings that night in Boyle City, hair down over her face, the blood of a compatriot dripping from her hands, the silent scream she offered up to the heavens as she ignored the bullets flying around her, none of those bullets, for whatever reason, touching her. Wouldn't Josiah Franklin piss himself if he had to face that? She hoped that she was around to see his fall. It was bad enough having to watch the end of her country, but for it to have been an inside job—that made her blood boil.

Bixby didn't want "justice." In her mind, wheelhouse justice was just a catchword with zero teeth. She wanted to be a part of the retribution.

She checked her watch again and moved faster until she was out of the tree line. If Maguire was right, and she always was, Bixby could walk up to the sheer cliff face at the map coordinates circled in grease ink and wait for someone to let her and the rest of the team in. She shook her head at the very prospect. Since when had anything gone according to plan? Bixby left the team behind at double time and followed her compass and map.

One Morrigan team member to meet one Cheyenne Mountain team member. Those were the compartmentalized orders: A one on one meet. She would have snorted out loud if it wouldn't have breeched protocol. *God it's cold.* But her feet kept moving. Many things ran through her mind as she covered ground, uneven, rough, and upward, and yet she still managed to do it silently, for the most part. She checked her watch again, and her compass, and the cliff face. It was getting close to time.

Her breathing came harder, visible in the colder air as she moved up in elevation. *I fucking hate the cold,* her brain reminded her. She shook her head. Mind games. Keep running, keep moving. Right, left, right left, cadence calls from past training units in her brain: *My girl is a vegetable, she lives in a hospital, I'll do anything to keep her alive...* She shook her head even as she chuckled inside. Gallows humor...ignore it. *I hear the choppers hovering, hovering overhead...come to get the wounded, come to get the dead...men at war...men at waar...*" Her feet kept moving.

Bixby skidded to a halt at the cliff face, almost slamming into it. She

checked her watch again. She was on time. Sweat dripped off her nose, chin, and forehead around her fucking beret.

The scraping sound of metal on rail and dirt grinding off to her right drew her attention to a heavy door that opened a crack. A long, pale face surrounded with short, red hair peered out.

"Sign."

"Morrigan," Bixby whispered, even as she subtly shifted her pistol forward.

"Currahee," came the countersign from the woman in an Air Force uniform. She shifted her body out of the narrow opening. "I'm Keough. Get them moving. We don't have a lot of time. Half hour to the next satellite flyover. An hour, maybe two, until the drugs wear off on the fucks inside."

Bixby laughed and settled her pistol back in its holster. "Great, another

fucking Irish."

Keough grinned. "My dad used to say, 'You can't swing a dead cat in the military without hitting a Mick.' It's better

204

than being a fecking traitor." She shrugged. "Call your team in."

Bixby chuckled and keyed her radio. "Charlie Two Two, Charlie One. Contact confirmed. Move in. Last one in, twenty-five mikes. Again, twenty-five mikes, absolute last. Over."

"Roger, read you clear. Twenty-five mikes last. How goes it?" Jennings asked. "Over."

Bixby keyed her mic. "Another fucking Irish." She sighed. "We might actually win. Over."

"That'd be nice for a change," Jennings drawled. "Moving now. Out."

Bixby released the com and looked back at Keough.

Keough grinned. "Welcome to Cheyenne Mountain."

THE END...FOR NOW

Author Roselle Graskey

Author Cheyne Curry

ABOUt tHE AUtHORS

Roselle Graskey is the author of October Echoes, October Echoes 2nd edition, Life's Little Edge and The End: Book One of The Sanctuary Series. She currently lives in Galveston, TX with her long-suffering wife Allison. Roselle is known for being a really tall child, watching hockey and trying not to take life too seriously. She is also not evil.

Cheyne Curry is the author of four published books, Renegade, Clandestine, The Tropic of Hunter and The End: Book One of the Sanctuary Series. She currently lives in the Midwest with her wife, Brenda, and their fur baby rescues Liam, Mesa and Belladonna Bossy Pants (the CEO of Bossy Pants Books). Cheyne, a former US Army Military Police Officer, was stationed in California and with the Southern European Task Force (SETAF) in Italy. Cheyne also co-writes, co-produces and composes music for short films at MP Grrlz Productions, her media company with Brenda. Cheyne has a background in law enforcement and entertainment security.

OTHER TITLES BY CHEYNE CURRY PREVIOUSLY PUBLISHED

Clandestine Tia Ramone is a gritty, self-destructive, ex-CIA operative who seeks absolution in a bottle. Jody Montgomery is a naïve heiress to a vast fortune, married to a man she discovers she really doesn't know. Tia's and Jody's paths cross in a sinister plot they are forced to take part in. With both their lives at stake, can the clandestine meeting that brought them together ultimately be the bond that saves them?

The Tropic of Hunter Hunter Roberge left Otter Falls, Vermont when she was 18, to get away from a life of scandal and judgment. Sixteen years later she returns to her 'hometown' for the funeral of the one person who condemned her the most: her mother. Being bequeathed the family house is just the first in a long line of mysteries that unravel the fabric of everything Hunter believes to be true. Can the support of a childhood acquaintance keep her on the right track or will she once again fall victim to her mother's hatred?

Renegade What would you do if one minute you were in the 21st century and the next you were in the 19th? One day you're driving a Mustang and the next day you're riding one? Dirty cop Trace Sheridan faces this dilemma as she moves from a present day mob war to a range war over a hundred years in the past. The year is 1879, when cattle barons, crooked lawmen, saloons, painted ladies, cowboys and Indians ruled the Wild West, and laws were only as strong as the gunman who upheld them. In Sagebrush, the town and the sheriff belong to the Cranes, who take what they want or bad things happen. Trace finds this out firsthand when she ends up on the land of Rachel Young, a struggling ranch woman who won't give in to the merciless cattle baron and his obsessed son. For some unexplainable reason, Rachel trusts the enigmatic Trace who uses 21st century sensibilities to battle 19th century turmoil, while Trace is forced to keep the secret of her origin from the attractive and vulnerable Rachel. Renegade is a story of redemption in its purest form as Trace discovers what truly matters in life and how past really is prologue.

OTHER TITLES WRITTEN BY ROSELLE GRASKEY:

October Echoes   Sara Pierson is a dedicated FBI agent, living and breathing her job. When a seven year old boy is kidnapped she pledges that the boy will see his mother's face again. She never expects the twists and turns the case provides, complicating things and making her job that much harder. Nora de Burgh is an Irish terrorist, in an American prison, with a long-ago tie to the boy's father. She has vowed to take her revenge - that the man is now a diplomat certainly complicates everything about the case. It's apparent that Nora has information that Sara needs from their first meeting - contacts in the Irish-American underworld, a culture that never forgets their history of hate and pain. Who are the good guys in the world of international politics? It's hard to tell and Sara begins to learn that fact the hard way. In order to find the boy and keep her promise, she must learn to trust a terrorist and along the way she learns that her black and white world has room for shades of gray. From Ireland to America and back again...both women find that the echoes of the past sometimes find the present.

Life's Little Edge   Callan O'Malley embodies everything that should scare Terri Barclay. O'Malley freelances as a gun runner for a biker gang, the dark secrets of her past influencing her present. Thrown together by circumstance and unexpected complications of living in the biker world, the women's lives are turned into chaos. Loyal friends of past and present, add to the mixture which brings the two women closer than they ever thought possible. Terri, however, is hiding her own secrets. Secrets that could very well get her--or O'Malley--killed. Terri must walk a fine line between what she now wants and what she is forced into by her sense of duty. She must redefine her approach on life and love and acknowledge that not everything is as black and white as she once believed. She soon discovers that living on the edge with a woman such as O'Malley can be an exciting yet dangerous place.

210

TITLES CO-AUTHORED BY ROSELLE GRASKEY AND CHEYNE CURRY:

The End – Book One of the Sanctuary Series

The power flickers, the ground shudders and when the backup system kicks in, Lieutenant Jessica Baumer and Staff Sergeant Branna Maguire do a routine equipment analysis and check the exterior surveillance cameras, where they see an unspeakable horror. Somehow, someway, without warning, the world as they know it has ended.

Originally used as 'lab rats' for an isolation experiment they are in their subterranean data center at Fort Hood, expecting another "normal" exercise. It becomes anything but.

There is little information available, which leads to many questions and no satisfactory answers. What happened and, more importantly, are there other survivors?

When the air begins to clear, Baumer and Maguire set off on a journey to one of the few areas of the country rumored to be less devastated by the attack. Their mission is to reach sanctuary, a safe compound and shelter run by a woman who has been preparing for a catastrophic event for years.

The law and order of modern day civilization has ceased to exist and the situation has become where only the strong and clever will make it to another day. Others join the two soldiers along the way; some are skilled, some are in need of rescue and others, who will stop at nothing to be masters of this new world order.

Do Baumer and Maguire, even with their military training, have the capability and fortitude to make it to sanctuary? And, if so, what will they find when they get there? Will it be the hope for civilization and America's future?

Or is this really The End?

COMING SOON
FROM
BOSSY PANTS BOOKS:

Permission To Recover (By Cheyne Curry): It's 1977 and Army CID agent, Lieutenant Dale Oakes is awaiting a medical discharge when she is reactivated by her former commanding officer and secret crush, Lieutenant-Colonel Anne Bishaye. Dale is planted into the first, experimental, co-ed OSUT (One Station Unit Training) company. Her assignment is to spend at least 16 weeks to expose who is setting up drill sergeants, giving the battalion a black eye. She and her undercover partner, Lt. Shannon Walker, get caught up in a whirlwind of unintentional intrigue while trying to keep their cover as new recruits and military law enforcement trainees. Dale discovers much more than is ever intended about the case and herself, as well. Can Dale and Shannon solve the mystery before time runs out?

www.ingramcontent.com/pod-product-compliance
Lightning Source LLC
Chambersburg PA
CBHW070456260626
47161CB00004B/1324